Moonkid

and

Liberty

• • • • • • • • • • • • • • • • • • • •

Moonkid
and
Liberty

• • • • • • • • • • • • • • • • • • • •

BY PAUL KROPP

Little, Brown and Company
BOSTON   TORONTO   LONDON

FIRST U.S. EDITION 1990

The characters and events in this book are fictitious. Any similarity to real
persons, living or dead, is coincidental and not intended by the author.

First published in Canada in 1988 by Stoddart Publishing Co. Limited

Library of Congress Cataloging-in-Publication Data

Kropp, Paul.
    Moonkid and Liberty/by Paul Kropp.
    p. cm.
    Summary: While Libby and Ian, who live with their nonconformist father,
experience the problems of starting over at a new high school, their mother
resurfaces in their lives and wants them to come and live with her in California.
    ISBN 0-316-50485-8
    [1. Moving, Household — Fiction. 2. High schools — Fiction.
3. Schools — Fiction. 4. Brothers and sisters — Fiction. 5. Divorce —
Fiction.] I. Title.
PZ7.K93Mo   1990
[Fic] — dc20   89-27192
                                                                        CIP
                                                                         AC

        10   9   8   7   6   5   4   3   2   1

Joy Street Books are published by Little, Brown and Company (Inc.).

HC

PRINTED IN THE UNITED STATES OF AMERICA

To Caitlin
and the real Ian:
Vale, vale

Moonkid

and

Liberty

1

. . . .

Libby

On the first day of school, I did not eat any of the five varieties of granola my father keeps in the kitchen. I cooked some eggs. This is part of a scheme that I came up with when we moved, a scheme to do something with myself. I figured I could begin with my body, trying to add some flesh to those places where nature had left me flat. Eggs are part of my scheme. So are English muffins with jelly. So are meat and potatoes and all the other normal foods that my brother Ian and my father refuse to touch.

"Are you actually going to eat those?" Ian asked as I put the fried eggs on my plate.

"Yeah. I'm going to try a normal breakfast. A human breakfast," I told him.

"You'll probably just get flabby like all the rest of them, Libby. Too much cholesterol, clogged veins, heart disease. Besides, a lot of guys like a woman who bears a close physical resemblance to a toothpick."

"Shut up, Ian."

"Those eggs, Libby. They're living beings — little

baby chicks who'll never make it to adulthood after what you did to them in the frying pan. They even look like eyeballs on your plate — see, with yellow pupils, staring at you."

"Don't try to gross me out," I said, breaking one yolk with my fork.

"There, you blinded it! Libby, you're a beast, a sadist," Ian said in that lecturing voice of his.

"And you're just weird. Now leave me alone or I'll throw my muffin at your deformed little face."

Ian grinned at me and ducked out of the kitchen before I could get a decent aim at him. I went back to eating my eggs, trying not to think about chicks and eyeballs.

Ian really was weird, of course. A few years ago, he got this idea that he was an alien abandoned on earth, destined for a mission that wasn't made clear to him. He tried to prove it to me one night by explaining that his ears are pointed, his head is too wide, and he is noticeably short for his age. But I knew he was just making an excuse because I had caught him talking to a fire hydrant as if it were a communication device to outer space. Ian wasn't an alien; he's just abnormal.

Unlike me. I was sick of being weird, strange, a toothpick, a joke. I felt I deserved a decent shot at some kind of normal life.

By the time I had eaten my breakfast and tried to put on a little makeup, my father, Rick, was finished with his morning meditation. He was standing at the door as Ian and I left for school, looking like the guys you see in magazine ads for "mystic consciousness." He never bothered to open his bookstore much before noon. In fact, the store had so few customers, I sometimes wondered why he bothered to open it at all.

"Now don't let them hassle you at the new school," Rick said. I'd heard that advice before, at every school we went to, and it never did any good.

"Yeah, yeah," I told him. I was busy looking through the closet for a coat that didn't scream out Salvation Army Thrift Store.

Ian had more to say, as always. "Hassles I can handle; harassment I reserve the right to protest." I could see that he was getting his vocabulary powered up for a big day at school. No wonder kids liked to beat him up.

"And don't be late getting back," my father said. "Your mother is calling today."

He didn't need to remind me, but Ian often forgot. For a kid who's supposed to be gifted, he has a lot of black holes in his mind that things can fall into.

"See you," I said, kissing Rick on the only bit of cheek that wasn't covered with beard.

My dad smiled. It was that wonderful middle-aged-hippie smile, which can stop babies from crying instantly and always manages to get a grin back from me.

It wasn't until we got out the door that I took a serious look at Ian. What I saw was embarrassing. My brother had dressed for his first day at a new school the way a workman might dress to put gutters on a house: gray, ratty running shoes, old cords with grease stains, a checkered shirt that had never, *ever* been pressed, and a jacket with a large number nine on the back.

"What are you staring at?" he asked.

"Ian, you look like some kind of slum kid."

"I *am* a slum kid," he shot back. "Look around, Libby. These aren't run-down mansions on our street, they're run-down bungalows. I mean, low is low."

"You still don't have to dress like where you come from," I told him.

"On the planet where I come from, I wouldn't be surprised if everyone walked around naked. So you think the way I look now is embarrassing, you should see me with my clothes off." Ian delivered this line with one of his stupider grins plastered on his face.

"Spare me."

"Then don't be such an obnoxious snot."

"I am not a snot," I said, frowning.

"You're working on it. All summer you've been getting ready to be a first-class snot. You'd think somebody with a name like Liberty would try to live up to it, but you're turning into a fashion slave like all the rest of them. I mean, look at the clothes on you. I don't think you ever owned a skirt before this summer. And I didn't know they made panty hose skinny enough for legs like yours."

"Stop being a jerk," I told him, ready to slug him if he kept on. "I just don't want this school to be a disaster like the last one. And maybe you should be worrying about it, too. It's the first day, Ian, and you ought to —"

"— put my best foot forward," he concluded for me.

"That's right."

"Did you ever see my best foot?" he asked. "Is it

ever ugly! Hammertoes. Must run in the family, because you've got them, too. So how am I supposed to put my best foot forward if I've only got the two miserable feet I was born with? Sometimes I'm amazed I can even walk."

"Ian, stop being so weird."

"What if I don't?"

"I'll tell everybody in this school what your middle name is."

"You wouldn't."

"I would," I said firmly, and that shut him up. Ian and I had both been cursed with weird middle names. Even my first name — Liberty — is bad enough. And my middle name is worse.

The school loomed up ahead of us, the only modern building for blocks around. It looked like a concrete block, windowless, gray — something like a military fort. I had been inside the week before to pick up my books, and I thought the lack of windows was scary. Maybe I'm claustrophobic. But I'd find a way to get over it. That's what I kept telling myself. I'm going to find some way to fit in here.

"Look at the gun turrets," Ian said, pointing up to where the architect had placed the school office.

"It's the design, Ian."

"Must be the same architects who designed the prison at Attica. They probably said, If it's good enough for convicted murderers, it's good enough for high school kids."

"Stop being paranoid."

"You'll see, Lib. Just try to sneak out before the end of the day and the guards up there will get you. Zap — you're gone. Laser weapons turn class-cutting students into plumes of smoke. The latest advance in education."

"Ian, stick the laser in your ear, will you?" Sometimes his crazy fantasies just make me tired.

We walked up to the concrete area just outside the front door. There were about thirty kids there, most of them taking the last few drags on cigarettes. A few were staring at us, or at least at Ian, since we were obviously new to the school.

I plastered a smile on my face and tried to look like I'd been walking through those front doors for the better part of my life.

Ian, of course, just held back and stared at all the kids. Something about the way he stares at people makes it seem like a challenge. And one kid took him up on it.

"Hey, you, number nine," the kid said, stomping on his cigarette. "Whatcha looking at?" There was a little laughter from the kid's friends.

"Nothing in particular," Ian said. "I was just wondering — is that your *real* nose?"

2

. . . .

Ian

In answer to the obvious earthling question, no, I did not have my head flattened on that particular morning.

What I find really appalling about you earthlings is that such a question pops immediately into your minds. I get harassed by one of your more primitive types, I reply honestly to him, and — *boom* — you immediately suspect that I'm going to be reduced to a rather small package of ground meat.

At least that's what Libby expected. She ducked inside the doors of the school so that she wouldn't have to see what happened next, the expected slaughter. She had seen enough of that in elementary school. But nothing happened this time. The school bell went off and reminded both of us — the bozo with the large nose and your resident alien — that we were not to spend the entire day loitering on the front steps. We had to go inside and be processed.

I told Libby that this new school would be just like the others. It really has nothing to do with the place itself — it relates to the function of schools in society.

Kids go in at age five or six, nice, innocent, weird little kids, full of energy and enthusiasm, ready to fight dragons or fly to the moon. Then, school. *Rrrrhyyyyyhzzzzzzzbangpop.* Out they come, drones at age eighteen, dull, interchangeable, fit only to consume heavily advertised products, work at dull jobs, and have babies. On any other planet, an institution that did this to its inhabitants would be regarded as barbaric. On Earth, we say all this is socially necessary and applaud the people like Mrs. H. Proctor who work at making the institution so effective.

Mrs. H. Proctor was the teacher assigned to look after my homeroom and teach us first-period English. I did not know, then, what the H stood for — maybe hydrogen as in H-bomb, maybe something awful like Hermione, or maybe H is the whole thing and she was simply the eighth child in a family that began with A. Proctor, B. Proctor, and so on.

With thoughts like these, perhaps it is not surprising that I did not hit it off with Mrs. H. Proctor.

"Let's check the roll," she began, smiling. "Albert Anderson?"

"Here," A.A. answered. That answer is part of the training, part of the process to stamp out the urge to kill dragons.

"Shannon Bidwell."

"Here."

"Amanda Capobianco."

"Here."

And so it went until she came to my name.

"Ian McNaughton," she said, still staring at the list. "Ian *Callisto* McNaughton?"

When the laughter died down, I answered, "That is my name."

"You have a most unusual middle name, Ian," she said. The class giggled again.

"Callisto is the fourth moon of Jupiter," I told her and the class. I did not tell them that I had already eliminated it as a possible home planet for yours truly.

"Oh, how interesting," she said, peering at me over the top of her glasses. I noticed that she had some lipstick on her left front tooth.

"Could I just ask," I went on, "why — of all the names on the list — you chose to read only *my* middle name?"

The rest of the class emitted an "ooh" to signify that I was challenging Mrs. H. Proctor's authority. The teacher gave me one of those aha-I-have-identified-the-class-troublemaker looks.

"Let's not start the year off on the wrong foot, Ian," she said.

It seemed to me I had heard a fairly similar metaphor on the way to school, but there was no sense getting into that discussion again. I prefer not to think about my feet, right or wrong, because of certain deformities in their appearance. I attribute these and other deformities to my alien birth. So did the student sitting behind me.

"Hey, Moonkid," he whispered.

"What?"

"Your face looks like dog puke."

I turned around to see who had managed to come up with this insightful aesthetic judgment. Perhaps I shouldn't have been surprised; it was the kid whose nose I had so richly insulted in front of the school.

I turned away from him and resolved to say nothing else for the time being. But I did make a mental note

9

on this person who had called me Moonkid. Not only was his nose quite large, but his whole face was vaguely Neanderthal — jutting jaw, sloping forehead, beady eyes. I mentally gave him the nickname Missing Link, but decided not to mention it to him immediately. I've found that earthlings don't take these things that well.

Fortunately, I am not an earthling, at least not a full-fledged one. I am an alien abandoned on a hostile planet. I came to this realization not long after my so-called mother went off to California to "find herself," as if somehow her self was lost in a place where she had never been. It was about then that I realized I bore no physical resemblance to either of my parents. In fact, I observed that I bore little resemblance to any earthling, save that most of my parts — mouth, ears, armpits — were in the right spots. Now perhaps it was possible that I was an incompetent son or an incompetent earthling, but I rejected those ideas. I decided I was a *very* competent alien who somehow had been left on this unfriendly planet called Earth.

Fortunately, I have had hints of life on my home planet. Every so often I seem to click out of this earth world for a few seconds, especially during videotapes in history class. This is obviously the time when part of me is checking in with my home planet. Also, I hold my pencil in a peculiar way — with four fingers. I suspect that on my home planet everyone has four fingers and it is only my imperfect earthling five-finger hand that is the problem. Finally, I found as early as the sixth grade that I am hopelessly attracted to girls with very large breasts. Since there are none of these in the sixth grade, and precious few older earthlings who qualify, this must be another clue to the nature of the beings on my home planet.

Neither Mrs. Proctor nor the class seemed disposed to treat aliens with kindness and compassion. I spent most of the period filling out forms, my four working fingers trying to produce legible print. No, there was not enough space to list all my previous schools. No, I have never been immunized against earthling diseases. No, I did not want a yearbook, activity card, discount-at-the-student-store package.

When the various forms were completed, Mrs. Proctor passed out a heavy green book called *Adventure Today.* The story she asked us to read was set in the nineteenth century, suggesting that the editors took "today" as a relatively broad period of time. Nor was there much adventure that I could appreciate, unless anguish in a Victorian drawing room gets *your* blood stirring. Perhaps it was not surprising, then, that the silent reading time led to little reading and a fair amount of noise.

It was almost the end of the period when I heard the whiz of a wad of paper flying by me, followed by a "Hey, man" from the girl who was its target.

Apparently I looked up just in time to appear guilty.

"Ian, did you throw that paper?" Mrs. H. Proctor asked, arching her eyebrows to produce that "troublemaker" look again.

"No," I said. I did a quick review of the trajectory and knew perfectly well that the paper had been thrown by Missing Link.

"You don't seem to be getting on very well for your first day here," she observed.

I ignored the accusation and said nothing. The rest

of the class, anxious to watch me get slaughtered, fell into a splendid silence. Mrs. H. Proctor stared at me. I stared at her. This continued until two girls quietly giggled.

"Would you be kind enough to pick up the paper for us?" Mrs. Proctor said at that point.

"I'd rather not," I replied, trying to be friendly but firm. "I think the person who threw it should pick it up."

"So do I," said Mrs. Proctor. I noticed a blood vessel in her neck beating visibly.

"Well, I didn't throw it. I don't do childish things like that."

"Perhaps you'll be an adult, then, and pick it up for all of us," she said.

"No," I replied.

"Then I think we'll just sit here until someone does pick it up," Mrs. H. Proctor decreed.

So we sat. The end-of-class bell went off, students began moving in the hall, and we sat. The earthlings in class all looked at me, or at the clock, or at their books. The paper sat on the floor. Mrs. H. Proctor glowered at me. Missing Link kept a look of perfect innocence on his face.

At last, a kid with glasses from the other side of the room — a kid who could not possibly, given the laws of physics, have tossed the paper — got up and threw the offending wad in the garbage can. Mrs. H. Proctor said thank you and dismissed us.

Suddenly freed, we rushed from the room. The kid with glasses came up to me in the hall as I was trying to find a stairway to the second floor.

"I'm R.T.," he said, as if a nickname like that made

any more sense than a real name like Callisto, "and I thought that whole thing was stupid."

"So did I," I told him.

"But you better watch out," he said to me. "I don't think that big guy likes you very much."

I thought that was a wonderful understatement, so I laughed.

"I can handle it," I said to R.T. "I've handled that kind of thing before."

All of that sounded quite brave, and I think R.T. was impressed. He at least risked his own skin by walking with me down the staircase to our next class.

And what I told him was the truth, I suppose. I've dealt with many kids who wanted to alter the shape of my face, or who felt my head would be improved with a few added lumps. This is simply what happens to aliens on a hostile planet, so we have to learn to handle it.

Unfortunately, we never learn to handle it *well*.

3
. . . .
Libby

The first day of my new life didn't quite measure up
to what I had in mind.

Nobody paid any attention to the new me. Maybe
I was better off than Ian, who was getting the wrong
kind of attention, but after all that effort, no one even
looked twice at me. In the old days, with my wild hair
and strange name, people at least knew who I was.
Now I felt like just one more body filling a desk. And
not even the desk of my choice.

I had left Ian in front of the school and made my
way up to 301, my English classroom. The teacher
was a balding man in a tweed coat and a rumpled shirt.
He was staring out the window as I came into the
room, maybe trying to imagine himself on a Scottish
moor. I went ahead and put my books on a desk where
nobody was sitting. I was about to sit down when
somebody spoke to me.

"Debbie sits there," the girl said, as if it would be
obvious to anybody.

"Oh," I said, and moved my books over to another
desk.

14

The girl who had lectured me on seating arrangements turned back to her friends, ignoring me as if I were some bag lady who had mistakenly walked in off the street. I sat down at the second desk and stared straight ahead.

"You're new," said a girl next to me.

Is it that obvious? I wondered.

"They call me Rabbit," the girl went on, as if the nickname were quite normal.

"I'm Libby."

"You'll like it here after a while," Rabbit told me. "Don't let Shelley and Debbie get you down. They're not like us."

I began to wonder what it meant to be like *us*.

"They call me Rabbit because of *this*," she said, smiling to show off her buck teeth.

"They call me Libby because it's my name," I told her.

Rabbit laughed. One nice thing about her is that it doesn't take much to make her laugh. That's something I figured out when class started. She was one of only two or three kids who laughed at the little stories the English teacher told. Rabbit was also one of those kids who put up their hands all the time. When Mr. Henson asked if anybody had bothered to open a book over the summer, it was Rabbit who recited a list of the novels she had polished off at her cottage in Maine. Most of the other kids looked bored at this recitation, so I tried not to be interested, either.

The most perfect bored look I have ever seen was on the face of a girl named Shelley Patterson, the one who had invisibly reserved a seat for her friend. Shelley managed to look alternately at the ceiling and at her nails in a way that said she was infinitely beyond

Rabbit and her summer reading list. I'm still not sure how she did it. She seemed to be slightly sighing with boredom and making a real effort at toleration, all at the same time.

Rabbit told me later that Shelley and her family owned not just one but *three* shopping malls. I think I was supposed to be impressed. And maybe I was, but it was more by what the money bought than where it came from. Shelley Patterson and Debbie Haskin and that group didn't dress in any really flashy style. But there was always one item — a watch, a sweater, a certain kind of haircut — that reeked of cash or style or travel or some flair the rest of us didn't have. Of course, I had no items that reeked of cash or style. I just had a bunch of items that reeked.

I said so, and that made Rabbit laugh. Rabbit's last name is McLeod, so in those classes where people sit alphabetically, she's automatically next to me. We ended up sitting next to each other in history class and we became lab partners in biology. It occurred to me at the end of day one that my automatic proximity to a social loser wasn't much help in starting a new life, but one friend has got to be better than no friends. The old Libby McNaughton spent too much time with no friends, trying to fill her life with butterfly collections or pet rats. The new Libby McNaughton would do better than that.

When I talked to my mother on the phone later that afternoon, I told her about the new me. I told her that I had bought some decent clothes with the money Granny gave me, that I'd had my hair done for the first time in my life, that I was going to be *somebody* for a change. I didn't tell her that nobody appreciated all the effort.

But even that began to improve by the end of the first week. For one thing, my weight was up by three pounds, thanks to my new, hefty breakfasts. Even if the three pounds didn't distribute just where I wanted them to go, they still made me look better. I took some more of Granny's money and went downtown to learn how to put on eye makeup. The lesson set me back thirty dollars, but I emerged with eyes that seemed larger than life. Just like Shelley Patterson's. Rabbit asked me why I wanted to look like a raccoon, but I thought I looked quite elegant.

So did Eddie Avery.

Let me tell you about Eddie. He was not one of the real movers and shakers in the school, not the kind of guy who could ever get close enough to Shelley or Debbie to smell their perfume, but he was good enough to be allowed an occasional seat in Shelley's sports car. Eddie has blond hair, nice eyes, and really high cheekbones. Rabbit says that if his cheekbones were any higher he wouldn't be able to see over them. Of course Rabbit doesn't like Eddie because he's a jock, but I wasn't so concerned about his collection of varsity letters. I just liked the idea that somebody male was actually paying attention to me.

"Hey, Libby. You got the answers to the review questions?" he asked me one morning.

"Sure," I said, smiling. I was trying to smile more — and at the right times. I figured this was one of them.

"Can I have 'em?"

"Any time."

"Thanks, Lib. Hey, did I ever tell you that I think you're okay?"

"No."

"Well, you're okay," he said, grinning at me.

This first encounter wasn't enough to make me melt on the spot, but it did make me feel warmer toward Eddie than I felt toward any other guy at school. Rabbit compared my state to that of butter on a summer day, not exactly melting, but easy enough to spread. Rabbit, may I say, was rabidly jealous.

Eddie made no further moves beyond borrowing my homework until the end of October. Then, exactly two days before the Halloween dance, Eddie came running up in a tracksuit while I was standing in the hall talking to Rabbit.

"Hey, there, Lib," was his opening line.

I smiled. By then, I had the smile down pat.

"I kind of wanted to talk to you about the dance."

"Oh," I said, giving Rabbit my best get-lost stare. She mumbled something and quickly disappeared.

"So you wanna go?" he asked me. The words didn't come out sounding very romantic, so I was a bit clueless.

"Uh, with you?"

"Yeah, sure," Eddie said.

"Well, okay," I said.

"All the guys are going," he said, looking around me as if all the guys might actually be watching. "So look, I'll come by your place about seven-thirty. Okay?"

"Sure," I said, trying not to smile *too* much. I didn't want to give it all away. I didn't want him to see anything on my face that might say this was the first real date of my entire life.

But Eddie wasn't looking. He raced down the hall, almost as fast as he had come up, and disappeared.

I was standing there in a daze when Rabbit came back.

"So he asked you to the dance?"

"Don't break the spell," I told her, my eyes shut tight. This was one of those moments in life I wanted to remember forever.

"I figured he was going to ask you out. He's had his eye on you in English for the last week. He's had that kind of look."

"You mean like he's hopelessly in love with me?" I asked.

"No, like he's horny."

Despite comments like that, I was still in a great mood when I got home that day. I was whistling, which is rare for me because I'm tone-deaf, and smiling like the cat in *Alice in Wonderland*. I got into the house, threw my books on the couch, watched some stuffing come out the hole in one cushion — and laughed.

I didn't even notice when Ian came in half an hour later. I probably would have ignored him altogether if there hadn't been an awful crash in the bathroom.

"What's going on?" I shouted.

"Nothing," Ian said. "Where's the Mercurochrome? How come we have fifteen kinds of organic food supplements and nothing to put on a cut?"

"Are you hurt?" I asked.

"Not exactly," Ian replied, sticking his head out the bathroom door. "I believe the expression for this is 'stomped,' as in the sentence 'I got stomped.' "

I wish I could say that I was surprised to see Ian all beaten up, but I wasn't. After the various slaughters in elementary school, nothing that could happen to Ian would surprise me. But I was a little concerned that he might be really hurt, like the time in the fifth grade when the kids actually broke his arm. I examined his face for damage. No footprints on the forehead, just a little blood around the nose and a few cuts on his forehead. "How'd it happen?"

"I think there were three of them, though I may have lost count after it got going."

"How'd it start?" I finally found some Bactine to spray on the cuts.

"How do these things always start?" he said, wincing as I sprayed his forehead.

"Usually your sarcasm gets somebody so mad they want to rip you to shreds," I said.

"Then you answered your own question."

"I want details."

"Okay, it went like this. I've been telling this kid I call Missing Link that he became extinct a hundred thousand years ago. I said he was an anachronism, but he didn't understand that, or maybe he thought it was some kind of venereal disease. Anyway, I asked him if he had an extra club and maybe we could go hunting for mastodons after school. For some reason, he didn't think it was funny."

"It wasn't funny," I said, simply enough. It was the kind of stupid crack that would make any normal person want to slug Ian.

"Maybe not, but even you would have laughed if you'd been there. Everybody else did."

"So he beat you up."

"With two or more assistants," Ian went on. "Whatever happened to the days of chivalry and the concept of a fair fight?"

"You're crazy."

"No, I'm an alien. And you know what, Libby? If

Missing Link is what it means to be human, then I'm *glad* I'm an alien."

For a second, it looked like Ian might actually break down and cry. I started to put my arm around his shoulder, but he tensed up and shrugged my arm off him. Maybe on his planet, no one ever needs a hug.

4

. . . .

Ian

Intelligence is a handicap, perhaps a worse handicap than being an alien. At least an alien knows why he's an outcast. Someone who's intelligent may be fooled into thinking he can actually get along with ordinary people.

That's a lie. A high IQ is a handicap almost like spina bifida or mental retardation. Yet all those people suffering from "official" handicaps have the law and five hundred government committees on their side. They have their own parking spaces, their own ramps, and more gallons of public sympathy than would fill a good-size wading pool.

What about us smart guys? I ask in the vocabulary of ordinary man. Did I ask to be born with an overly efficient brain in my head? Did I ask to be crippled with a large vocabulary? Do I really want to spend my life condemned to books and libraries while normal people are watching TV or out having a drink with the guys?

Absolutely not. I even considered a lobotomy at

one time, but then I read what it does to one's sex life. So now I demand justice, not for aliens, but for anyone crippled by excessive folds in the cerebral cortex. We want to be like anyone else. We want to be able to run for student council and have a chance, some chance, any chance, of winning. We want to be able to say the dumb things that real men belch out in beer commercials. We want to go out with the girls in those beer commercials.

Is that too much to ask?

Probably.

What does it have to do with the fact that Missing Link beat me up?

A great deal.

One of the worst problems about being an intelligent kid is that certain low-forehead types will necessarily hate me. There will be many who merely despise me for being brighter than they are, but then there are the few who hate me for my brains in a basic, natural way, much as dogs hate cats. Why? I don't know why. On my planet, things don't work like that. But here on Earth, I seem to spend a good deal of my time trying to keep my brain from being stomped into mashed potatoes.

It was the second week of school when Missing Link managed to get me. I even had a warning beforehand.

"Don is going to pound you out after school," announced one of the round-faced kids in my math class.

"Oh? Missing Link is getting aggressive again?" I said.

"He says you bugged him in English."

"That's not true," I said. In fact, I had merely

laughed when he mispronounced a word during some oral reading. The laugh just came out — I couldn't help it. I even offered him the right pronunciation, but that just seemed to make matters worse.

"Are you gonna fight him?" the kid asked.

"I can barely reach his head with my arms extended," I replied. That was something of an exaggeration, but not much.

"Yeah, but are you gonna fight him?"

"Only if I receive an engraved invitation."

I believe an attitude like this is referred to as "chicken" by most earthlings. Why humans take a rational attitude — avoiding personal injury — and describe it with an animal term I have no idea. Perhaps slaughter and suicide are inbred in earthling genes. Given the history of the planet, I wouldn't be surprised.

"You're not going to fight Missing Link, are you?" said my one friend, R. T. Meinhardt. He was called R.T., I had discovered, because his first name, Rudolph, had been taken by a reindeer sometime before he was born.

"It wouldn't be a fight," I said.

"Yeah?"

"It would be suicide."

"A massacre," R.T. agreed.

"Technically, a massacre involves more than one person. Now if you wanted to join in . . ."

"Not me. No way," R.T. exclaimed, staring at me as if I were a madman.

Some earthlings might get upset if their friends failed to stand by them at a time like this, perhaps because earthlings assume that friendship should take precedence over intelligence. Well, I disagree.

I thought it courageous enough for R.T. to accompany me down Leinster Street after school. He even offered to take my body to a funeral home when it was over. And I appreciated that.

"He's going to get you in the alley," R.T. explained.

"What alley?"

"The alley where they always have fights."

I wondered if there was a sign to designate the spot — FIGHTS HERE — the way some other alley might be marked NO LOITERING.

"So let's avoid the alley," I said, always sensible.

"Then he'll get you behind the store."

"So we'll go the other way."

"Then he'll get you in the woods behind the elementary school."

Little did I know that the neighborhood was set up as a maze with no exits for us mice who'd rather not fight our way to the cheese. R.T., who had had some experience in being beaten up himself, suggested I take the alley. He explained that there the actual beating could only last so long before someone would call the cops. Behind the store or in the woods, a guy could theoretically be pummeled forever.

"This is stupid," I said as we came up to the alley.

I think R.T. probably agreed with me, since he almost always agrees with me, but he was too scared to say so. Up in front of us were three of Missing Link's lieutenants: a boy named Carl, who smiled in a mildly retarded fashion; a kid named Marco, who was relatively small, as in my size; and a guy named Bobby, who had outgrown his diminutive name.

"Where you going?" they asked me.

"Home," I said.

"Don wants to see you."

"Tell Missing Link to make an appointment with my secretary."

"Smart ass, eh?"

I couldn't disagree with that. Libby says I actually enjoy being a smart ass. What I didn't enjoy was the pushing and shoving that followed.

This wasn't exactly a fight. I was merely trying to get by. Missing Link's buddies were merely trying to bring me into the alley. Needless to say, I ended up in the alley.

"I've been waiting, Moonkid," Missing Link said to me. He was smiling, like a cartoon cat with four fingers wrapped firmly around a mouse.

"Oh," I said. I think even I was beginning to get a little upset, since my usual clever patter wasn't coming forth.

"Well, come on," Missing Link said and proceeded to cuff me in the face.

Now an earthling fight is an interesting affair, especially for those of us from other planets. If I were parked in my spaceship overhead, the scene below would look like a target. The crowd of kids made a circle of bodies around the bull's-eye of the target. The bull's-eye itself consisted of Missing Link and me. From a spaceship, the visual effect would be quite lovely.

Unfortunately, I was not getting the spaceship view. I got the view from the center — and this was much less attractive. I observed a wall of kids, all of whom wanted my usual pink and white skin tones changed to black and blue. I saw Missing Link looming across from me. I say looming because he is actually quite a bit larger than I, perhaps six extra inches in height and twenty pounds in weight. For a moment, I thought it might be to my advantage to mention this difference in size so that the proposed fight would look like an act of cowardice on his part. I thought this twist of earthling logic might stop the whole thing.

But I never got the chance. Missing Link just hit me again.

This made the crowd go slightly berserk, as if I were a Christian, Missing Link a lion, and they the Roman populace. I've never thought much of the Roman or any other populace.

"What's the point of this?" I asked, refusing to defend myself.

The logic was lost. He hit me again.

It was at that point I lost control. Every so often I fear that my parentage is mixed — part alien, part human. If so, it was the human part that acted from that point on.

I laced into Missing Link with both fists flying. He fought back, slower but with more strength. The blows and counterblows were moving so fast that it seems blurred even in my memory. I do recall trying to get away at one point and being hit by Marco. I also recall being picked up by R.T., who told me I was doing very well, considering.

But at the end, all I remember was Missing Link sitting on my chest, punching my face.

Someone must have come out of a house at this point, because there was some loud shouting in heavy ethnic, sort of "You kidsa get outa here!" The voice was enough to cause both the lions and the populace to disperse. I think this would have been quite interesting to see from the spaceship view. But from where

27

I was lying at the time, I couldn't properly appreciate it.

After Missing Link and the others had disappeared, I was left with R.T. and the man who had saved my face from a closer resemblance to Silly Putty. The man bent over me and asked in heavy garlic breath whether I was all right, to which I replied yeah, though that was not entirely truthful.

To be entirely truthful, I hurt all over. To be entirely, entirely truthful, I was a bloody mess.

Maybe Missing Link had even inflicted some cortical damage, because when R.T. helped me to my feet, there was only one thought in my mind. It wasn't an alien thought. It wasn't even an intellectual thought.

It was simple earthling: I wanted revenge.

5

. . . .

Libby

By dinnertime on Halloween night, I was in a panic. Eddie was coming to pick me up at seven-thirty, but I knew I'd never be ready. The doorbell kept ringing with little kids who wanted treats. But my father was meditating, and Ian was doing something equally useless downstairs.

"Do I have to do everything myself around here?" I shouted when the doorbell jangled for the umpteenth time.

Ian came strolling up from the basement, where I think he'd been hiding. "Nice costume," he said.

"You really think so?" I asked, amazed to hear anything pleasant from him.

"Yeah. You really look like a prostitute," he said.

"I'm supposed to be a princess," I told him.

"Oh. Well, maybe you should work on it some more and I'll handle the beggars."

At least the second thing he said sounded good. I headed off to the bathroom and tried to figure out what was wrong with the costume. Rabbit had helped me pick it out down at the Salvation Army — a really tacky, gauzy dress that looked right out of *The Wizard of Oz*. The dress would be perfect, we thought, to make me a princess.

I tried putting some glitter on my eyelids. Blink, blink. There. A lot more princesslike.

"How's that?" I asked Ian when I came downstairs.

"I don't know, Libby. Maybe the real you just isn't a princess," Ian said.

I groaned. There was a time when Ian and I used to back each other up. When my mom left and Rick went to trial and everything went crazy, we were pretty much all each other had left. But then Ian decided he was an alien on some strange assignment to Earth. His comments about my personal appearance became more and more sarcastic, as if the beings on *his* planet were born with acid tongues.

Why did I even bother to ask what he thought about my costume?

I went into the living room and stumbled over my father doing a *pranayana* on the middle of the floor. I just about wanted to die. He had told me he was going to be out; otherwise I would never have agreed when Eddie said he would pick me up at the house. But there he sat, a thirty-seven-year-old man sitting cross-legged on the floor, staring straight ahead, his whole brain focused on breathing. No wonder everybody thought we were weird.

"Rick," I said.

No answer. He had that look of a man who had reduced his pulse rate to fifty beats a minute — sort of half dead.

"Rick!" I shouted, pushing harder at what remained of his consciousness.

He opened his eyes and looked at me. "Shh."

"I haven't got time to shush," I told him. "Look, my date is going to show up any minute and I've got enough troubles without you looking like some crazy swami on the living room floor."

"Libby," he said, blinking his eyes, "why are you hassling me?"

"Because I want you to look a little respectable when Eddie shows up." This seemed a pretty dumb idea when I looked at him. Rick was dressed in one of his Indian cotton outfits, like a Gandhi hand-me-down. Why are parents so embarrassing?

"Would I be more respectable dressed in a Brooks Brothers suit and smoking a pipe?" he asked me, standing up.

"I don't want to get into another fight," I told him. "I've got enough trouble already with this costume."

"I think you have a very convincing costume, whatever it's supposed to be," he said.

"I'm supposed to be a *princess!*" I shouted, loud enough for even Ian to hear. "Now look, I've got a date coming to the door in a couple of minutes. Me, a date, my very first date ever. And I don't want to spend the whole evening explaining —"

There was a knock at the front door with no trick-or-treat after it. I froze. The knock came again.

Eddie!

"I'm not ready," I whispered to my father. I had to check myself in the mirror again. My eyes weren't made up. My bra straps weren't pinned. I didn't have any choice but to get Rick's help.

"Can you get the door?"

My father nodded and I ran to the top of the stairs. There was a third knock and then I heard the door

31

open. I peeked downstairs to see if it was Eddie, and it was — dressed as Count Dracula.

"Good eeevening," Eddie said, trying hard at a Transylvanian accent.

"Hello," Rick said in that mellow voice of his. "Are you Eddie?"

"Yes, sir," Eddie told him. "I like that costume of yours. I guess you must be going out, too."

"As a matter of fact, I am," my father said. "Come on inside. Libby will be right down."

My father was doing all right, but I didn't trust him to keep up the front for long. I took one quick look in the bathroom mirror, fixed my eyes and my dress, then sprinted down the stairs.

"Eddie," I said, out of breath.

"You ready to go?" he asked me.

"Yeah, sure," I told him. I wanted to get him out of the house, out where my father couldn't do anything to embarrass me.

But I wasn't fast enough. "Libby, just hold on for a minute," Rick said, disappearing up the stairs.

"We don't want to be late," I shouted to him. He'd been doing so well, pretending to be normal. What was he going to do now?

Eddie just stood there, sort of fidgety. I said something about how nice he looked. He said something about how nice I looked. Then we ran out of things to say.

After a few awkward moments of silence, my father reappeared. He had a magic wand in his hand. It was left over from one Halloween when Ian had dressed up as a wizard.

"To complete the princess," my father explained, handing me the wand.

"A princess?" Eddie said. "Now I see it!"

"You just needed the whole outfit," Rick replied.

I smiled. Sometimes my father tried so hard it was enough to make you cry.

"What time does she have to be back, sir?" Eddie asked. It seemed funny for anybody to call him sir.

"Time?" Rick said. I don't think he'd ever thought about a curfew before. All our lives he just asked Ian and me to be reasonable. Maybe that was the toughest curfew of all, but Eddie would never understand.

"The usual time," I said, trying to cue my father.

"That's right. The usual time," Rick said, playing along.

Then I aimed Eddie out the door, winking at my father for playing his role so well. So far, so good. Now just let the night go well — let everything be normal. Please. Please.

Eddie didn't have a car, so we walked to the school. That was fine by me. I was enjoying the cold, clear air and the scattered bunches of trick-or-treaters still hitting up houses for candy. Eddie seemed so dashing in his tuxedo that I could ignore the fangs. I thought he looked wonderful.

"I feel happy tonight," I told Eddie.

"Yeah?"

"Like things are finally starting to go my way."

"You bet," he said, putting his arm around my waist, pulling me close just for a second.

We got to the front door of the school and made it past the teachers guarding the entrance. My English teacher was over at one side, staring at the ceiling as if he were a tourist at the Sistine Chapel. My math teacher was standing by the coatroom, dressed in a clown suit. He seemed to be sniffing all

33

the kids who came in to see if they were obviously boozed up.

I said hi to the clown and dropped off my sweater with Eddie's Dracula cape. Then we went into the gym and danced.

Now most of the time I'm something of a klutz when it comes to anything physical. I'm the kind of person who drops teacups or trips down stairs. But tonight was different. I danced like I really knew how to dance. Maybe other kids *were* looking at me, maybe my hands *were* dripping with sweat, but I was all right. Eddie liked me. Eddie was laughing and smiling, asking to dance one more. So why not? Why not be normal and enjoy it?

It was sometime after eleven when I made my way past the crowds and into the girls' washroom. The place had a layer of smoke starting at shoulder level, like some sort of killer fog. I ignored the smoke and the general mess, only stopping for a second by the mirror to make sure my makeup wasn't running all over my face.

"Nice costume, Lib," said the girl next to me. It was Debbie Haskin, who moved in Shelley Patterson's group.

"Thanks," I said. I was amazed. Debbie Haskin had never said a word to me since the first day of school.

"What are you supposed to be?" The question didn't seem to be very important to her, but it made me nervous. Where had I put my wand?

"Uh, what do I look like?"

"A teenage hooker," she said, as if it were obvious. "But you need more makeup. Right now you look too much like Snow White, you know?"

I smiled stupidly. This was getting out of hand.

"Shelley and a bunch of us are going over to the El Morocco after the dance. Maybe you and Eddie want to come," she said, packing makeup back into her purse.

"Me?" I couldn't believe it.

"You and Eddie. Snow White and Dracula."

"Well, sure. Thanks."

"Just watch your throat," Debbie said. "Dracula's fangs can leave a real hickey." With that, she crushed her cigarette and went off.

"Uh, thanks again," I said to her back. Then I felt dumb for thanking her so much. Why was I so amazed that Shelley's group — *the* group — should ask us to come along with them? Because it was a miracle, that's why.

Maybe I should explain that I have never, in my whole life, actually belonged to anything. It seems to me that I've spent my whole life looking at all the kids who fit in, all the ones who belong, from the other side of a pane of glass, like a poor kid with his nose pressed to a department store window. I guess it was partly because we moved so much that it was hard to join anything. But there was more to it than that. It had something to do with my father and the way our little, lopsided family never seemed to fit in wherever we lived. I mean, once I was even rejected by the Girl Scouts. It wasn't that I wouldn't have bought the uniform or learned how to tie the knots; it was that my family was too different. No daughter of a hippie rabbit farmer was going to go once a week to church with the nice girls. Not in Elmira, anyway.

But this wasn't Elmira anymore. Debbie had given me a chance to join Shelley and the others. She had *invited* me to join them!

I was more than just bubbling over when I got back to Eddie. I think it might be better to say that I was like a Coke can that somebody has been shaking up and down. I was ready to explode.

We got a ride out to the El Morocco with Bill Moore, his girlfriend, and two other kids from school. We all packed into the little Toyota, practically sitting on top of each other. The ride out gave Eddie an opportunity to grab at me more than I wanted, but it seemed to make him happy. As for me, I was flying anyhow.

Debbie and Shelley were already at a table when we got to the restaurant. Shelley was sitting next to the gorgeous guy I had seen her with at the dance. Eddie told me that the gorgeous guy was named Bob and he was old, like twenty-five, and did something in photography, but I wasn't concentrating much on the details. Everything that night had a glow, an aura. The details got lost in the color.

The waiter finally came around and everybody ordered drinks, and that all seemed to go just fine until he came to me. It suddenly occurred to me that I had never, ever ordered a drink before. Panic. What had Shelley ordered? I couldn't remember. Where was the menu? Nowhere.

"I . . . uh, a locust," I said.

"Excuse me?" the waiter said, arching his brows.

"I mean a grasshopper." That was it. I had heard that in a movie once.

"Could I see your ID, please?" the waiter said.

"ID?" Was I ever starting to feel stupid. "I, uh, I haven't got my purse." A good lie on the spur of the moment.

"She's all right," Shelley said to him.

The waiter nodded and went on to ask Eddie what he wanted. I looked over at Shelley and gave her a smile to say thanks.

We must have been a strange-looking crew, sitting in the restaurant in our costumes. Shelley was dressed as a vampire with a black wig and a slinky black dress. Debbie was Raggedy Ann and her date was Raggedy Andy. The rest of us, if I remember, were a clown, a pirate, two Roman centurions, a car-crash victim, Dracula, and me. Whatever I was.

We sat there talking and laughing, mostly about school and the dance and the nerds who weren't with us. The drinks kept on coming, round after round, and things just got funnier and funnier. Maybe that's what it's like to be on the inside of things.

Then the food came, some chicken wings and ribs. I don't remember who ordered any of it, or how it was paid for, or even if I ate any of it. But I do remember the wine that came with it. I remember the way it warmed my stomach and made me feel even sillier than before, sillier than I had ever been in my life. The wine made a little campfire deep inside me, sending up smoke to cloud my brain. No wonder everything glowed.

"You want to eat any of these?" Eddie asked me. I think he was offering me a chicken wing, but I had trouble seeing it.

"I don't wanna eat," I said. At the time, I thought the words were perfectly clear. "I wanna drink."

"Well, sure," he said, filling my wineglass again.

I drank that glass and I was still all right. My speech was a little slurred and my brain was a little smoky, but I was fine. Everyone at the table seemed so good-looking, so witty, so charming, so intelligent. And I belonged with people like that, if only to appreciate their genius. And I was fine . . .

Until the Spanish coffees. I don't know exactly what's in a Spanish coffee and I don't remember asking for a Spanish coffee, but somehow a mug full of the stuff appeared in front of each of us. Was I supposed to just let it sit there, unappreciated, untried? No. I drank the steaming fluid, saying something about needing coffee to sober up.

Then it hit. The Spanish part of the Spanish coffee got to my stomach and my brain at the same time. The campfire in my stomach suddenly flared up, like somebody had thrown in fireworks. The smoke came up and made my brain dizzy. I had never been so dizzy.

I got up without saying a word, my hands perspiring, my eyes watering. *Bathroom* was the only thought in my mind. *Get to the bathroom.*

"Are you all right?" Debbie asked me.

"Fine," I said, lying like crazy. I was dizzy and sick and hopeless. One more word out of my mouth and everything, everything would have come out with it.

Somehow I steered myself to the bathroom, the guck in my stomach moving in waves as I walked. I reached the bathroom and oh, oh, was I sick! In the toilet, on the floor, on my nice princess dress.

But I could handle all that, really I could.

What I couldn't handle was when I got up off my knees and turned around. Debbie and Shelley Patterson had followed me into the bathroom. They had seen everything.

6

· · · · · · · · ·

Ian

Halloween is when earthlings show their true nature. They throw away the mask of reason and display the real beast that lies underneath. The beast takes many forms — animal, devil, goblin. Sometimes earthlings try to deny the beast, like Libby dressing up as a princess. But it's there. It's part of earthling nature.

How do I know? Observation. Have you ever seen a little kid dress up as Galileo or Mahatma Gandhi or Desmond Tutu? Not a chance. The inner life of earthlings has nothing to do with the noble causes some few extraordinary people work for; the inner life of earthlings is mired in death, violence, and fear.

Beam me up, please. I've finished my research. I'm ready to go home.

On Halloween night, Libby went off with some sixteen-year-old jock who hardly seemed worth all the worrying and carrying on. Libby was embarrassed by my father, as if she would have preferred to be born into the same family as Beaver Cleaver. I think my sister is getting many of her ideas of normality from watching television, a machine we managed to do without until Granny handed us one with the house. This machine is apparently what earthlings use to socialize the young. No wonder Libby and I turned out so peculiar, growing up without the magic box. I never realized that real life was punctuated with laughter every twenty seconds, that all problems could be neatly solved in twenty-two minutes, and that any tense situation was cause for a commercial break. I guess I never knew what life was all about, as someone on a soap might say.

Libby seems to have found out quickly enough. This new, fatter image of herself strikes me as hopelessly conformist. I preferred Libby as she used to be, sort of mangy but with an idea or two flapping around her brain and Gertrude, her pet rat, crawling up her arm. That was when she actually deserved the name Liberty.

These days Libby seems to be more of an aspiring airhead, though perhaps I am exaggerating. My father says I'm misjudging Libby, that we have to let her develop her own "space," one of those old hippie words for letting her do what she wants. Of course, my idea of space is something else altogether.

On that particular Halloween night, my father stayed at the house just long enough to embarrass Libby and provide two dozen home-baked granola cookies to kids who really wanted gooey chocolate bars. Then he went off to see his girlfriend, Margaret, a woman who bears such a remarkable resemblance to a string bean that sometimes I call her by the appropriate Latin name, *Phaseolus vulgaris*.

I settled back on my favorite beanbag chair and

turned on the television to watch *Night of the Living Dead,* a black-and-white classic where dead people rise up to start eating the living. Of course, aliens are immune to the kind of cheap terror that affects most earthlings. Being alone in the house on Halloween and watching a horror movie on TV did not affect me at all.

But the noises outside did. At first, all I heard was a tick at the side window. I didn't think much of it. Windows tick all the time, don't they? Houses settle on their foundations, the glass contracts, there is a tick. Nothing to be disturbed about.

Until the second tick. This time I went over to the window and looked outside. Nothing at all. I turned away from the glass and there was another tick, this time sharp and distinct. I knew right away that something had been thrown against the glass and bounced off.

Earthlings, I thought. Next comes the soap. Poor Mrs. Johnson next door will be looking at the soap until next summer, at the rate my father cleans things.

I went back to my movie and thought more about Halloween. It comes from Saturnalia, of course, "an occasion of unrestrained or orgiastic revelry and licentiousness." I wondered how soaping windows connected with ancient rites involving wine and sex. Sometimes I think these earthlings are in a state of historical decline.

The house was quiet for about five minutes, except for the action on TV. On the small screen, the living dead were gathering outside the farmhouse, pushing at the boarded windows to get at the people inside.

Suddenly there was a pounding at our front door.

41

I jumped up, half from the real sound, half from the events on television. It was too late for tricks and treats, or at least for treats. So I tiptoed to the front door as silently as I could on the creaky floors. It was quiet for a while. Then the knocking came again.

I threw open the door. Nobody there.

I stepped out on the little concrete slab at the front of the house and looked around. The wind was cold as it blew against me, but there was nobody in sight.

"I know you're out there," I said to the kids I couldn't see. No sense letting them think I didn't know what was going on. No sense letting them think I was afraid.

I went back to the television in time to watch a dead little girl suddenly sit up and kill her mother. Gruesome. Then the knocking started again.

I didn't move.

The knocking got louder. The ticks at the window were back. I began to worry about the glass cracking and how that could be explained to Granny.

At that point, I actually thought about getting help. I might have called the police, saying something mature and sensible like "This has gone far enough." Or I might have phoned my father at Vulgaris's house and asked the two of them to do their *Kama Sutras* over here.

But I didn't get the chance. The lights in the house went out. The TV set clicked off, leaving only a tiny dot of light in the center of the screen.

This is a good trick, I thought, *a very good trick.*

There were two things to do at this point. I could either rush out and attack or stay inside the house and deal with whatever might happen next. I thought about attack, but judging from the simultaneous ticks and knocks, there were at least two of them. The odds were bad.

So I made a strategic retreat. I figured my room upstairs was a better place for defense than the living room. To get up there, they'd have to make it past my father's stacked rabbit hutches in the hall, his bags of rice in the kitchen, and a lethal throw rug, which had tossed me more than once. All in pitch black.

I felt my way to the hall and up the stairway to the second floor. My bedroom was at the left. I felt my way along, touched the Albert Einstein poster on the door, and went in. I fell down on the futon and felt, for a moment, secure.

Then I heard the door open downstairs. It was easy enough to do since my father was philosophically opposed to locks. There was no way I could keep anybody out.

I began to imagine what was going on down on the first floor. I pictured an invasion of Mongolian dwarfs, scurrying all over the floor. Hundreds of them. Vile dwarfs eating the beanbags, engaging in orgies atop the rice, stuffing themselves with granola.

Then there was a tremendous crash and a shout of pain. I knew it was the pile of rabbit hutches. Booby trap number one had caught one of them. Now if only they'd retreat.

"Ian."

I didn't say a word. I didn't move. I'm not sure I was even breathing.

"Ian . . ." A different voice.

"Eee-an . . ." A third voice.

They kept calling out my name, moving around

below. Their voices were strange, mixing high and low tones. Eee-an. Eee-an.

They were searching for me in the darkness, stumbling over the beanbags and the clutter, but still searching. In a minute they'd realize I wasn't down there. Then what?

I heard them come out to the hall. Now they knew where I was hiding.

"We're coming to get you, Ian."

"We know you're up there."

"We're going to smash you, Moonkid!"

The last voice I knew. Missing Link. Maybe it was the sound of his gruff voice that snapped me out of my stupor. Suddenly I realized that this was not just a trick, that it would be another beating. With no one around to stop it this time.

The three of them were coming up the stairs. Slowly, feeling their way in the dark. They didn't know which bedroom. That gave me time.

Time to plan. I went slowly to my closet and found a flashlight. That gave me light. A quick look inside gave me an idea, something better than a weapon. It was a monster's mask.

"We hear you, Moonkid," Missing Link's voice said. He was on the second floor now. Close, too close.

I heard my bedroom door open. But I was ready — the mask was on my face, the flashlight in my hand. The room was still in total darkness as the three of them felt their way inside.

I let them get closer, closer. Only surprise was on my side. I could hear the breathing. Closer. Closer still.

It was time. Quickly I kicked out with my foot,

44

catching one of them in the leg just as I turned on the flashlight. My mask was lit by the beam, and its hideous face glowed in the pitch-dark room.

I screamed.

The kid I kicked screamed.

Missing Link and Marco screamed.

Then they were running, fighting each other to get out of the room. I kept screaming at the top of my lungs, trying to sound like something from another world.

They ran. The first of them fell down a bunch of stairs. The others didn't stop. They must have stepped on him in their rush to get out.

Their cries moved downstairs and out of the house, dropping in tone like a train whistle in the distance. From my window I watched them leave. The last one out was Missing Link, dragging one leg behind him.

I smiled, then caught myself. Smiling was an earthling thing to do. Besides, this wasn't the end of it. Perhaps I had got some peace for the rest of Halloween, but that was only one night. Surely they'd wake up to what I had done and feel like the idiots they actually were. Then, by some peculiar twist of earthling logic, they'd be after me again. And the next time I had to be ready for them.

7

· · · · · · · · ·

Libby

When the taxi brought me home from the El Morocco,
I didn't notice that the lights in the house weren't on.
I didn't notice much of anything. The taxi driver
brought Eddie and me to the front of the house and
waited. The question of a good-night kiss flashed
through my dim brain for a second, but nothing came
of it. After the disgrace I had made of myself, I knew
why.

I staggered into the house and flipped the light
switch. No power. I figured my father had forgotten
to pay the bill again. I groped forward in the dark,
hit my foot against a rabbit hutch, felt my way up the
stairs, and climbed into bed.

There I died. Or almost died. I have no idea how
I knew a perfectly black room was spinning around.
But I knew, and it was. Nothing was standing still.
Nothing at all. The room was a black, spinning hole
that sucked me inside to die. Or at least to sleep.

The next morning was Saturday. That meant I didn't
have to face everybody at school. In fact, I didn't feel

like facing anybody at home, either. I stayed in bed until eleven, when some guy from the electric company put up a ladder outside my bedroom. This seemed to make an incredible amount of noise, so I got up, still feeling woozy. I stumbled against Gertrude's old cage and almost fell face first into my butterfly collection. Two relics of the old me. I just wished that the new me didn't feel quite so sick.

Rabbit called. "How was it?" she asked. I guess she hadn't heard yet. "Was it divine?"

"Well . . ." I said.

"Well what?"

"The dance was pretty good and then we went to El Morocco," I told her. That much was the truth. I wondered how much of the truth I wanted to spill. My head still didn't feel very good, sort of fragile.

"You and Eddie?" Rabbit asked, sounding like some kind of gossip reporter.

"Me and Eddie and some kids," I said, since Rabbit thought Shelley and Debbie were snobs.

"So did you have a good time? What did you eat? What did Eddie say? Did he make any moves? Look, I want to know everything," Rabbit insisted.

"Everything?" The end flashed in my mind — the vomiting, the toilet, Debbie's voice.

"Yeah, if it isn't too kinky to tell me."

"I — I had a great . . . No, I didn't," I said, breaking down. "I ruined everything."

"What?"

I was crying now, so the words didn't make any sense when they came out. "I got so sick . . . I had to throw up, because of the coffee. It was Spanish. I couldn't help it . . . and they found me in the john

47

and had to take me home." I kept thinking about that look on Shelley's face. *The girl can't hold her drinks. Maybe she's more of a loser than we thought.*

"Oh, Libby. It must have been awful," Rabbit said. She was good with sympathy.

"Worse than awful."

"But it's not the end of the world," Rabbit went on in that sickening, cheerful voice of hers. "I remember at Melanie's party, I was so sick. I told my father it was the pizza, but I knew he could smell it on me."

"Yeah, I guess." I was thinking of ordinary fathers, of Ward Cleaver, who always seemed to know what Buddy was doing. Why couldn't I have one of those instead of a bearded ex-hippie, ex-draft dodger, ex-everything?

"How did Eddie take it?"

"I don't know. I mean, there wasn't any big fight or anything when he brought me home, but . . ."

"But what?"

"Well, you know. Nothing happened."

"You expect him to sweep you off your feet when you smell like barf? Come on, Libby, get real. You were doing okay until you got sick, so what's the big deal? I bet he'll call you today to say that he's sorry for getting you drunk."

"Really?"

"Sure. Just wait for the phone to ring. It'll be him."

Rabbit said this with all the certainty of somebody who's never had a date in her life. When Rabbit hung up, I tried to believe all the encouraging things she said. And maybe she was right. Maybe Eddie would call.

Waiting for the phone to ring isn't easy. It's not as

if you can sit right by the thing, ready for it, because that would be too stupid. But I tried to make sure that I was never far away from it. I'd be doing something quite sensible, like making dinner, but all the time I'd be watching the phone from the corner of my eye. I even checked the line to make sure that nobody had cut our phone service. After what Ian's friends did to the electrical wires, there's no telling what other jerky stuff they might have had in mind. But all I got was a dial tone when I checked. The ring was nowhere.

My father came in from the bookstore at six and seemed glad to find me out of bed. He asked me one or two questions about last night, then politely steered conversation in another direction. That's one thing I like about him: he doesn't jump on you when you're down.

"Good day at the store," he told us when we sat down to eat. "Sold the Camus journals off the back wall."

"Who'd want to read the diary of a camel?" I said.

"No, Albert Camus, *his* journals," Rick explained. "When I ordered them two months ago, the salesman thought I was crazy. But I knew that somebody would come in and buy something like that. Some of my customers have got real taste in literature."

"Amazing that they come into the store," Ian mumbled.

Rick just looked at him. I think he was hurt by the comment.

"All I meant was that a window display on life in Albania — the socialist paradise — is hardly something to bring intellectuals into your bookstore," Ian went on. "You've got to advertise to the customers you want to reach."

"But Albania, that's a matter of conscience," Rick said. "I'm trying to educate the people here."

"You don't educate people through a store window, Rick," I said, joining Ian though it felt funny being on his side.

"You can educate people anywhere, one step at a time," my father replied.

"Then you ought to have TV ads and bus posters and a radio jingle," Ian went on. "Comm-u-nism, there's no life like it. Comm-u-nism," he sang.

"Albania is an independent socialist country," Rick lectured.

"Don't be cynical, Ian," I added.

"I'm just taking Rick's idea to its logical conclusion," Ian shot back.

"Whose logic?" I asked him.

"My logic."

"Obnoxious, twelve-year-old logic."

"I happen to be thirteen, Libby."

"Well, it doesn't show."

"And I suppose your performance last night was adult, eh?"

Rick came in to save me from embarrassment. He said something about how important it was for the three of us to support one another. Ian snorted and looked at the ceiling. I kept eating, hoping that somehow the vegetarian food would make me feel better. But I didn't get far into the eggplant.

The phone rang. Eddie! I was up like a shot, racing into the living room. I could have lifted the receiver by the second ring, but I realized that it would seem like I'd been waiting by the phone. I paused. Two more rings. Then, in my most controlled voice, I said, "Hello."

"Libby, it's Mom," came the voice on the phone.

I was stunned, maybe disappointed. It's not that I didn't enjoy talking to my mother; it's just that she wasn't Eddie. Get hold of yourself, Libby.

"Oh, hi," I said. "How come you're calling on Saturday?" It was a sensible question. Usually she called us during the week so the long-distance charge from San Francisco was absorbed by the television station where she worked.

"I couldn't wait till Monday. I just got the tickets today."

"Tickets?"

"I've got plane tickets for you and Ian. I want you to come out and visit us over Christmas. What do you think about that? Wouldn't that be wonderful?"

"Well, I guess." I hadn't seen my mom in five years, not since the police raided Rick's health food store and she ran off to California. We had talked. She had written. But I hadn't visited her for all that time because there never seemed to be enough money to go.

"I want you to meet Michael and see how we live now. And I want to see you. I mean, you're all grown up and we've never had a chance . . ."

Her voice dropped off. She gets pretty emotional on the phone sometimes, so I tried to help her out.

"Ian's right here," I said. "Why don't you tell him about it?"

"Sure," she said.

I pulled back from the receiver and called out to Ian. "It's Mom. She wants to talk to you."

"Sharon?" Ian asked.

"We do have the same mother," I said to him, handing over the phone.

I walked back to the table, my mind spinning. Rick must have seen the confused look on my face.

"What did Sharon want?" he asked me.

"Us," I said.

"What?"

"Ian and me, for Christmas," I explained. "She's already bought the tickets."

"Well, how about that," my father said. The look on his face was kind of stunned, as if someone had called to say we'd won a lottery or been selected for the first civilian flight to Mars. I suppose the look on my face must have been pretty much the same. I began to wonder if the phone call had been real or just some weird part of my awful hangover.

Until Ian came back, scowling. "Sharon wants to talk to you," he said to Rick.

My father went off, leaving Ian and me and three plates of cold eggplant parmigiana.

"I think our so-called mother is showing off some of her big bucks," Ian muttered.

"Why do you always have to be so cynical?" I snapped back. "She's our mother and she wants to see us. That's called *natural,* Ian. That's called *human.*"

He just raised his eyebrows and stared at me with a weird expression on his face. At that moment, Ian didn't look very human at all — he looked like a real moonkid.

8

. . . .

Ian

Libby was enthusiastic; I was skeptical. I suppose these two different responses to my mother's fly-to-California proposal were predictable. Libby has always been overjoyed to receive any of the crumbs that Sharon might want to dust off her emotional table. I find it hard to get excited about crumbs.

Neither of us had seen her for five years, a period of motherhood she had marked with a dozen letters and a few phone calls. Sharon had left when the police busted Rick's health food store in Elmira. The charge against my father was drug dealing, though it was based on a small marijuana patch in our back garden. In fact, my father was a granola-and-rice dealer, which probably made him even more detestable in the eyes of the good citizens of Elmira. My father did not want their suburban split levels, their four-wheel-drive Jeep Wagoneers, their Little League baseball games.

At some level, I think my mother did.

Anyway, the police trashed Rick's store and managed to mess up his life for a good year. It was during that year that Sharon left, explaining to us through several gallons of tears that she had "lost herself" in marrying our father, that they had not "grown together."

Sharon went off to California, where she hoped to "find herself," I suppose. Instead she found a salesman for Nucrotech named Ted, an EST zombie named Richard, and a horny professor whose name I've forgotten. There was also an artist named Nick, a period of time in Venice, and two years of university mixed in with everything else. And I suspect there was more, since all I know is what she was prepared to admit in print or on the phone.

After such a checkered history, perhaps the most astonishing thing about her invitation is that she was actually able to pull it off. Obviously she was now capable of assembling the couple of thousand dollars required, calling a travel agent, and having a place to live that could be predicted two months in advance. For once in her life, everything seemed under control. She'd greet us at the airport. Don't worry about expenses. Tickets will arrive in the mail. Sharon sounded as competent as any legal secretary at Crunch, Murfield and Gotlieb.

Even before she left us, I had some questions about whether Sharon was actually my mother. Now I realize that, genetically and sexually, it is the father's role that is usually in doubt. But I can see *some* basic resemblances between my father and me, at least in attitude and personality. I see absolutely no similarity between Sharon and myself. If I am of mixed alien-earthling birth, I suspect it is my mother's genetic portion that was replaced. If so, then this woman who calls herself my mother really has no more than a nostalgic claim on the position, and relinquished any actual rights five years ago.

Those were the thoughts I took with me to bed. Libby and Rick seemed convinced that I was going to California, that it would be bordering on the lunatic to do anything else, and that the matter was settled. I did not think the matter was settled, but I had other things to worry about. There was, of course, Missing Link, who was certainly figuring some further means of revenge against me. There was Mrs. H. Proctor, who was threatening to have me declared gifted so some special-education types could throw extra work on me. There was a vice principal who had already lectured me on my "insolent attitude" after a brief altercation with Marco in the cafeteria.

And there was my body, which was growing in the most peculiar way. The left side of it seemed to be lengthening more than the right, giving a lopsided quality to the whole torso. What if this continued? Should I see a doctor now or did this happen to all aliens?

I used to be able to talk to Libby about these things, but lately she seemed off in a world to which I hadn't been assigned. After her Halloween orgy, she'd told me one or two things about what happened, mostly about the "divine" time she had had. I told her one or two things about my Halloween, though I left out Missing Link's entry into the house. In a peculiar way, we were talking to each other but not really saying anything. I was busy emphasizing my intelligence and clever thinking. She was trying to emphasize her beauty and social acceptance. When we finished talking, I had a hunch we both were lying through our teeth.

On Sunday morning, I was slurping down a bowl of granola when my father came out to the kitchen.

"Ian, I've been thinking," he began. I didn't doubt that for a minute. At one time, my father had been quite a brilliant student, though he'd never quite been able to finish college.

"Thinking about what?"

"About the window display. The one on Albania. Perhaps the bookstore is being too aggressive in giving it a whole window, just like you were saying. I was thinking if we got more people into the store —"

"Then you hit them with Albania when they least expect it," I broke in.

"Well, something like that," he said. "I don't want you to think I'm selling out." He looked at me, dead serious.

"I don't think changing a window display is selling out," I told him. "It's a matter of tactics. You don't see a million people marching for peace anymore, do you? But that doesn't mean the goal isn't there."

"Yeah, that's right." He nodded. "I think a little more subtlety, a little broader audience, and maybe that's the way to make it work. This past week, I counted the people who came into the store. One hundred and twenty-eight customers, and I knew them all. I felt like I was running a club and not a bookstore."

"So you're actually ready to take Albania out of the window?" I asked him.

"Yeah. Maybe you could give me a hand today and

we'll put up a new display." He smiled. I had a hunch he was smiling the same way Galileo did when he told the pope, No, I'm wrong, the earth really is the center of the universe. Sometimes it's hard to tell when someone is smiling and when he's gritting his teeth.

I grabbed a few things out of the house — spray paint, aluminum foil, some paper from art class — and went off with Rick. It was a beautiful Sunday morning and we were both feeling good. Rick started talking about seeing God, somehow, by meditating about tree bark, and I didn't even bother to argue. It was that nice a day — until we came to the store.

"Looks like they soaped your windows a day late," I said as we came up to it.

"I cleaned most of it yesterday. This is new," Rick told me.

The windows were so soaped, in fact, that they were basically white. We couldn't see much of the Albania display or anything else inside the store.

Until Rick opened the door.

The place was a disaster. Books were on the floor, some with pages ripped out, blowing from the wind we let in. The back door was open, its window broken. A spray-paint message was underneath the broken window. The message simplified our politics to "Commie" and our sexual practices to one word more.

My father muttered something I couldn't hear; then he looked at what had been his life-in-Albania window display. The pictures of happy proletarian farmers had been ripped and crumpled; the map of Albania was full of punched holes. The books on

Communist life, all of them, had been soaped and spray-painted.

I bent over and picked up one book, a nice hardcover that still looked in pretty good shape. I opened it up and found that the pages had been X'd with a knife.

Rick was at the back, in the literature section, which was largely untouched. I walked back to comment on that, to say that the damage wasn't all that bad. But I was too late. My father was crying.

I pretended I didn't notice and went over to close the back door. Then I began picking garbage off the floor, stuffing it in a bag from the little storage room. By the time I reached the front, where the real damage was, Rick was all right again.

"Well, let's look on the bright side," I said. "You'd already decided to change the window display, so all they really did was get you started." I sounded like Libby, sort of fake but cheerful.

"It'll take months to replace those books," my father muttered.

"Well, you never sold any of them, anyway."

"That's not the point," he shouted, suddenly angry, but not at me. The emotions were all confused.

I nodded and went back to cleaning up. In a minute, Rick was beside me, his arm around my shoulder.

"Sorry, Ian," he said, his voice a little cracked.

"It's okay," I told him, throwing a mutilated hardcover into the garbage. "Maybe you should let me do this part and you can start sweeping up."

"You're right. I'm too angry to handle this right now."

That made two of us who were angry. For my father,

it was a general anger against a society that didn't want to listen or read or think, against a world that was aggressive in its stupidity. For me, it was more direct. I knew who had done this, even if I could never prove it to the police. Scratched in the soap was a name I'd heard before — Moonkid — a name used only by one particularly dense group of earthlings.

9

Libby

That Sunday after Halloween was probably the lowest point in all our lives. My father kept on mumbling to himself about "fascists" and "not selling out." Ian was exhausted from cleaning up the store all day and seemed nervous, as if he expected somebody to jump out of the closets at him. And me? Well, I was dead. I had died Friday night — romantically, socially, personally, and any other way that counted. It felt like the day after the drug bust back in Elmira, the day that finally drove my mother away.

Ian seemed to have gone right off the deep end. He got back from the bookstore and immediately began putting a lock on the front door. He had a kind of shell-shocked look on his face, and jumped when I came around front and tried the lock. I guess that's his weird form of depression.

But my father was in the worst shape. He just couldn't get over the vandalism to the store. It wasn't the damage so much as the unfairness that got him depressed. The bunch of kids who wrecked the front of the store had stuck a pin in the balloon of my father's dream. Rick didn't run a bookstore; he ran a dream store in an ideal world. That night he sat cross-legged on his mat, looking sad and a little pathetic.

I went in and knelt down beside him.

"It was bad?" I asked him. At that point, I hadn't seen the damage to the store.

"Bad," he said simply. When my father is most upset, he tends to have the least to say. He's pretty much the exact opposite of Ian.

"You can't let some stupid vandalism get you down," I told him, trying to sound more cheerful than I felt. "You can get the store fixed up again."

"But why should I?" he asked.

"Because you believe in it," I said. "All of it — books and socialism and Albania and everything else. It's your whole life."

"That's what I was wondering about." Rick cast his eyes down at the mat. "Sharon seems to be doing so well now, and we're just hanging on here —"

"Dad, we're not moving again," I said firmly.

"No, I wasn't thinking of that," he replied. "I was just . . . well, when I went to the store, I wanted to get a book for your trip. You know, I wanted something like a Michelin travel guide to California. So when I was cleaning up the mess, I kept looking for something like that, saying to myself, 'What kind of bookstore doesn't even have a simple travel book?'"

"It doesn't matter."

My father looked up at me, his eyes brightening. "Well, I did bring you something," he said, "though it's not quite what I was looking for."

He uncrossed his legs and got up from the floor.

Over on the bookshelf was a wrinkled supermarket bag, which he brought over to me. Inside was my father's going-away gift: *Endangered Sea Life Off the California Coast.*

"It was the best I could do."

"Oh, Rick," I said, giving him a hug. "It's a wonderful book —" and then I couldn't say any more. I think if I'd tried to say any more, I'd have started crying, and then maybe Rick would have started too, and then Ian would have come in and looked at us as if we were just a couple idiotic, emotional earthlings. So I fell silent, and we had this moment together holding the book and each other.

Next morning, the most amazing thing happened when I got to school.

Eddie talked to me! It wasn't a really warm, easy conversation, but who cares? He said he was sorry that I ended up "getting sick." And then he gave me that shy little smile of his, and I had to smile back. I wanted to kiss him right there in the middle of the hall, and maybe, just maybe, he felt the same way. Of course we didn't do anything, not then, but I had a grin on my face going into math first period. And that grin didn't quit all morning.

At lunch there was a second miracle. I was eating lunch with Rabbit, telling her that maybe things weren't quite as hopeless with Eddie as I had thought, when I saw Shelley Patterson on the other side of the cafeteria. She was looking around for somebody, so I hid my eyes and tried to become invisible.

"What's the matter with you?" Rabbit asked me.

"I'm not here," I said, hiding.

"Of course you're here."

"I don't want Shelley Patterson to see me, not after what happened," I said.

"All you did was get drunk," Rabbit said. She was always so practical.

"I got sick — all over — and she had to clean me up. I wanted to die."

"Well, you might want to die again. She's coming this way."

I ventured a look up and saw that Rabbit was right: Shelley was coming to our table. What was I going to say?

"Recovered?" Shelley asked me. She was grinning that perfect smile of hers.

"Kind of," I said.

"Well, it happens," she said, tossing off the whole thing in three words. "Listen, we're ditching last class and going shopping on Wednesday. You interested?"

I almost choked. "Shopping?"

"Cleo's," she said, as if it were obvious to anybody. "There's a sale and I've had my eye on a Harvey Fraser. Daddy says I have to go to the Armory Ball this year or else."

"Oh, of course," I said, as if that meant something, as if the social calendar were printed indelibly on my brain. "I'd love to come."

"Meet us in the parking lot. Debbie's driving. And you might want to bring your dad's credit card, just in case you see something."

"Well, sure," I said, as Shelley waved herself off.

Rabbit just stared at me. She had a look on her face like *I* was some kind of alien.

"Cleo's?" Rabbit said archly. "You can't afford K mart."

"Well, there's a sale."

"Bring your dad's credit card? Do they have any idea who your father is?"

"You don't have to be rich to have a credit card," I said, though it would never have occurred to Rick to apply for one.

"Are you sure you can afford to mix with that crowd?"

"I'm just going shopping, going along for the ride."

"Yeah, sure," Rabbit said, packing up her lunch. "Just watch out how far the ride is going to take you."

Rabbit was jealous, of course, but there wasn't much I could do about that. If she wanted to get her nose out of joint just because Shelley asked me to go shopping with the group, well, that was her problem.

My problem was simpler: cash. Wouldn't it be great if I could actually buy something at Cleo's sale? After all, I was going to California and I didn't have any clothes for that, either. The more I thought about it, the more convinced I was that I deserved some money for new clothes.

I took the bus over to Granny's right after school. She lived on the other side of town in a huge old house, which she had split up into apartments. Granny lived on the first floor, in an apartment that was about as big as our whole house. Of course, she had the money to live anyplace she wanted. My grandfather had been an optician who plowed most of his money into real estate. When he died, Granny found herself owning a dozen houses, including the one we live in. Granny had turned most of the houses into apartments and become one of the major landlords in the city. That was her last rational act. Then came the cats.

Granny began with one cat, Sam. By the time Sam was finally wiped out by a truck, there were Reginald, Kitty, Rufus, and Sam Jr. Then Sam Two appeared at her doorstep, and Sam Three, as well as Angelica, Reggie, Tabby, and dozens of others whose names I'd never know. Granny looked after them all, supporting two veterinarians and the Humane Society as well.

I had to step over a half-dozen sleeping cats in the hall before I could knock on Granny's door. One of them, a black one, began to curl around my leg. I wondered if that was an omen.

The door was answered not by Granny but by Rick.

"What are you doing here?" I asked him.

"Borrowing money," he said. Sometimes my father's honesty was just embarrassing. "What about you?"

"Well, uh, I just wanted to talk to Granny for a minute," I mumbled.

"Let her in, Richard. Let her in," Granny ordered as she came bolting out of the living room. She was followed by a troop of cats that somehow managed to avoid being stepped on. "Libby, you come right in and sit down. I've had quite enough of your father and his bad news, so I could use someone to cheer me up. Would you like some tea? Or a drink? Are you old enough to drink now, dear?"

"Well, uh . . ."

"Now, Richard, you just get on your way. Libby and I have some things to talk about, woman to woman. And I've done all that I can for you. Now scoot," she said, shooing my father away as she might an overly large tomcat.

My father grabbed his old pea jacket and wrapped

his scarf several times around his neck. "I'll come by and see you next week," he said.

"I'm not sure I can afford to see you once a week, dear. But do call," she said to Rick as they went down the hall. She closed the door behind him, then turned to me.

"Now, Libby, did you say you wanted a drink? Of course, the tea is already made. Could I pour you —"

A bright orange cat began climbing up Granny's pants leg and distracted her from what could have been a monologue. It was because of the monologues that Ian couldn't stand her, but Granny's speeches didn't bother me. All I had to do was say yes or do-you-really-think-so once or twice and she could carry the show for an hour.

"Now, Libby, I must say you are looking a bit better than when last I saw you. It's nice to see you filling out. You just tell your brother that he won't be small forever. The McNaughtons are all late bloomers, even your father. I don't think he had a whisker on his face until he was twenty, and now look at him. Sometimes I think —"

"Uh, Granny, I really can't stay that long. It's my night to cook supper."

"Oh, of course, Libby. Now if that mother of yours . . . but that's another story and perhaps she's not to blame. Your father was part of that mess, too, and perhaps it was the nature of the times —"

"It's really about clothes," I said, sipping the luke-warm tea.

"Your father never did know anything about clothes. I don't think I've seen that man in anything but blue jeans for the last twenty years. And to think

66

that his father, when he died, had a closetful of suits and ties. I almost cried when I had to give all those to the Salvation Army. But your father —"

"Well, it's *my* clothes I'm worried about."

"But if I remember, and I may be getting senile but I do remember things, I thought I gave you some money just two months ago and you —"

"Well, I did. You see, these clothes are some of what I bought," I explained. "But now, well, I have a chance to visit my mom over Christmas."

"I doubt that your mother will be able to stay in one place long enough for you to find her." Granny reached over to stop a black cat from clawing at her ankles.

I went on, ignoring the swipe at my mother. "Anyway, I need some clothes to wear."

"To California? They wear shorts out there, I thought. When I look at television the girls are wearing next to nothing —"

I wasn't being convincing. This would end up nowhere unless I came up with something fast. "Well, there's another thing. I'm going to the Armory Ball and I need a dress." I just blurted it out. It wasn't a terrible lie, just a little one.

"The ball?" Granny said, looking impressed.

"I won't need much money. There's a sale at Cleo's so I think a hundred dollars would do it."

"One hundred dollars!" she said. "Do you know that when your grandfather set up his practice he made only one hundred dollars in the entire first year of work?"

Actually I *had* heard that story before, though the dollar figure varied with Granny's memory.

"It's inflation, Granny. Clothes have gotten very

expensive. I really can't go to the ball in my school outfits."

"Well, of course not. You are a McNaughton, Libby, and have to dress appropriately."

"So I thought —"

"Don't say one word more," she ordered. "You've been given a wonderful opportunity and I'm going to see to it that you can go to it splendidly. Here. My checkbook is still here from bailing out your father again. If I can do something as silly as rebuild a bookstore, I can certainly buy you a dress. It might be nice, really nice, to have one other person in the family end up respectable. Lord knows, I've given up hoping for your father."

As Granny scribbled out a check, I managed to get one cat off my lap and two others away from my feet. I wondered if cats came with respectability.

"There, buy a dress and some nice shoes and whatever else you need."

"Thanks, Granny. This is important to me." Three cats jumped away as I stood up to give her a kiss.

"I know," Granny said. "I remember being your age. That was when I met your grandfather," Granny began, and continued talking as I made my way to the door.

It wasn't until I got to the hall that I looked down at the check. There was my name and there was the amount: $250. Two hundred and fifty dollars! I'd never had so much money in my entire life.

I stuck the check in my purse and looked down at the black cat rubbing against my leg. I could be wrong about this, but I swear that the cat was smiling back at me.

10

· · · · · · · ·

Ian

Recent changes in Libby, even before the new clothes, have been quite dramatic. I attribute all of them to sex. Earthlings, you see, are literally dominated by their sexual drives. This madness extends from some time in early adolescence, say twelve, to the point where they approach senility, say twenty-nine. During this period, earthlings allow their sex drive to determine such basic items as their appearance, their behavior, their achievement in school, their life goals, their every waking and perhaps every sleeping moment. I find this astonishing.

For aliens such as myself, the vague lure of a girl with large breasts may well be important, but it would never interfere with basic functioning. Eating, thinking, reading sci-fi, and drawing pictures — all this must go on regardless.

But earthlings! Here is a race of creatures who consider themselves civilized. They have inherited a philosophical tradition going back almost three thousand years. They live in a complex society that is so tightly interconnected that a new fertilizer in Germany applied to corn in Iowa will change auto production in Japan. But these people, these "civilized" people, can be individually disabled by a suitably seductive smile.

Consider my sister. Libby cons $250 cash from Granny, enough one-dollar bills to swell several of my pockets. She has enough to buy a good bicycle, ten art pads, five good novels, and the collected works of Marcus Aurelius — and still have money left over for a granola bar or two. But what does Libby do? She buys clothes. She buys a sweater for $75. My father's last *car* only cost $75. And that sweater, the $75 sweater, does exactly the same job as my Sears $17.95-on-sale-for-$14.95 sweater, except that Libby's has a label with someone's name on it.

And Libby bought makeup. This was not just the odd cream to cover a zit, but *makeup*. This was makeup designed to coordinate with her skin, to color the areas around her eyes in layers, to make her lips visible from a quarter mile away. Why? The answer, ladies and gentlemen, humans and aliens, is sex. In this case, Eddie.

I did not see the full effect of the $250 until perhaps a week after the purchases were made. I did see Eddie come to the door, and noticed that he had made no particular effort to improve either his wardrobe or his face. Nonetheless, when Libby glided down the stairs in *the* clothes with *the* makeup, the look in Eddie's eyes showed that all the expenditure was having the desired effect.

Libby seemed to feel herself transformed. She treated poor Eddie like some hopeless admirer who

70

would do until the appropriate prince showed up. It seemed to me that the new look had had some transforming effect on her personality, her very mode of thought.

Now this is where I draw the line. I rather liked my sister when she was younger, when she didn't mind being called Liberty. That was when she went to school all ratty and feisty, ready to pound out kids in the playground who were twice her size. I liked the way she took our poverty-stricken and socially outcast state and wore it like a badge of honor. That was the sister I wanted to remember, the crazy tomboy who collected butterflies and liked nothing better than dissecting worms and lizards — not this made-up, sexually driven female.

It is one thing to set up one's body to be physically attractive; it is another to reconstruct the mind to do the same thing. Now Libby's brain has never been a particularly wonderful instrument, but it has never been crippled before, either. These days I see it in a definite decline. She introduces words and phrases with "like." She's begun reading *Cosmopolitan,* articles like "How to Dump Him After Your One-Night Stand." In short, Libby has begun to trash herself intellectually. Her brain is starving from self-induced dieting. *Anorexia intelligensia.*

"Ian, go sit on it," Libby replied when I brought the matter up.

"I only mentioned it because I'm concerned."

"And Rick only mentions it because he thinks every woman should look like Vulgaris. The two of you are living in prehistoric times. Rice-bag dresses and scrubbed faces went out before any of *us* were born."

"Who's us?" I asked her.

"Shelley, Debbie, me, other people you wouldn't know."

"They're all a bunch of snot heads, Libby. They walk around with their noses so stuck up it's like they got hung up on an invisible clothesline. Those kids don't think, they don't —"

"Ian, those *kids,* as you call them, are so far beyond you that they scarcely know you exist. Frankly, I'd like to keep it that way."

"You're becoming just like them," I threw at her.

"It's about time" was all she would say.

Apparently my efforts with Libby were doomed to failure. Once sex becomes the dominant drive, the call of reason is pushed back and even ridiculed. Of course, I should be used to that. Ridicule was something I had tolerated since pretty early on in my life; it comes with having a middle name like Callisto. But lately I was accepting less of it. I was becoming, in my own way, a little more aggressive.

The object of this aggression was obvious: Missing Link. He appeared in school on the Monday after Halloween with his leg in a cast. Obviously his fall down my stairs had taken a toll. Also obvious, to me, was that he and his gang had gotten revenge against my father's bookstore. I suppose the matter could have been called even at that point and the two of us might have gone on to live fairly normal lives. But I wasn't satisfied with that. I wanted to teach Missing Link and his group that alien life forms should be left alone. I wanted them to confess, to suffer, to cry out in pain. Some days my urge for revenge was so great that I became convinced my earthling half was taking over.

My first act of vengeance was remarkably childish, and it embarrasses me to talk about it. R.T. had brought in a tube of instant glue for a project he was working on. I was trying the stuff on my fingers before class, noting that instant really meant two minutes, when the idea came to me. Somehow, I couldn't resist the temptation.

Missing Link hobbled into the room and I quickly spread a line of the glue on his seat. He suspected nothing. But I knew it was his day to get up and do homework on the board. I also knew that the glue would be set by that point.

When his huge bulk attempted to rise up, his jeans were firmly stuck to the seat.

Rrrrip!

What I hadn't anticipated was just how much everyone else would laugh. It was uncontrollable. Missing Link turned red and hobbled off. Mrs. H. Proctor scolded, stamped her foot, even yelled. But the laughter wouldn't stop. Peachy Martin fell out of his desk and laughed on the floor, tears running down his pink cheeks. Crazy Zuckerman stood up and did an imitation of Missing Link, hands to his rear, and the laughter came in a new wave.

Of course I had to laugh, with all the rest of them, for cover. But I wasn't laughing inside. The thing was too stupid, too small. What I wanted was something larger. I wanted to take Missing Link's pride and pulverize it, like a teacup dropped from the World Trade Center. I wanted him in smithereens. The glue was nothing. A futile exercise that only made my life worse.

I was sitting in my front-row seat, conveniently removed from Missing Link's back-row desk, smiling my most innocent smile, when the wrath of Mrs. H. Proctor descended upon me.

"Ian," she said in a fierce whisper, "I want to talk to you after school."

The other kids were still giggling about Missing Link, so Mrs. Proctor's words did not elicit the usual "oooh." No one seemed to notice, except me. And I smiled and looked ignorant, a difficult feat for me in the best of circumstances.

At the end of the day, I returned to Mrs. H. Proctor's classroom and stood in front of her desk until her last class was thoroughly cleared out. I figured that standing was better than sitting, since it suggested a short interview.

Mrs. H. Proctor thought otherwise. "Sit down, Ian," she said. She was peering at me over the top of the half-glasses she wears to read.

"Yes, ma'am."

"I don't suppose you know anything about what happened to Donald this morning."

"No, ma'am. I thought it was very juvenile." The second sentence was truthful, at least.

"Only a few of your classmates would be capable of pulling off that stunt," she told me.

I had to smile. "Kids learn a great deal from movies today, Mrs. Proctor. The values in a film like *Porky's Revenge* lead to just what happened in class. In fact, I was reading an article in *Harper's* just the other day about the effects of media on young people."

"I'm sure you were," she said, frowning. "Ian, let's stop this verbal fencing. I *know* you did it."

"But —"

"No buts, Ian. I know perfectly well that the stunt

was part of some continuing silly war between you and Donald. I just want you to realize that," she said, taking off her glasses. "I know."

I wasn't sure what to say, so I just stared back. I swallowed, but something seemed to catch in my throat.

"This episode is symptomatic, Ian," she went on. "Symptomatic?"

"Don't pretend you don't know the word," she said, turning to me. "I've seen your files and I've got the test results. Don't ever play dumb with me, young man. You have a problem."

"What's that?" I asked. I knew that part of my problem had left school without the seat of his pants. And I knew that some of my problem was at home and some in California. And I knew that most of my problem was being an alien. But there was no sense admitting any of that.

"You aren't willing to fit in," Mrs. H. Proctor announced as if this were some great insight.

"Oh."

"You have ability, talent, intelligence — and you won't share it. I put you in a group and you fool around. I ask the class a question and you answer in ways none of them can understand. You have no friends and seem to enjoy being an outsider."

"I am an outsider, ma'am. But I do have friends."

"Oh, yes, poor little R. T. Meinhardt, who thinks the sun rises and sets with you. But worshipers are not friends, Ian. You have tremendous abilities, but you'll get nowhere unless you learn to cooperate."

These heavy clichés led me to raise one eyebrow. I think it was my right eyebrow.

"Don't act like that, young man. Your superior attitude is part of the problem and it's going to stop right now. Or else."

Ah, she was cornered. "Or else what?" I said.

For a moment, Mrs. H. Proctor was at a total loss. But then an awful grin came to her face. "Or else I'll make you Donald's tutor. The school says we can take our best students and assign them to help children who, well, need extra help. How'd you like to work with Donald every day in the library conference room? How do you think that would work out?"

I shook my head. Missing Link and me locked away together every day. He'd break every bone in my body, all two hundred and fourteen of them, one each day.

"So you're going to learn how to cooperate, Ian. You're going to learn that you may be different from the rest of us, but you're not better. You're going to participate. You're going to stop this attitude of superiority. You're going to treat me and everyone else in this class with respect."

She stopped for breath. I waited for the obvious conclusion.

"Or else."

11

. . . .

Libby

Shelley and Debbie wanted to drive me to the airport at Christmas, but I had to say no since Rick was so stubborn about taking us. Besides, Ian didn't want to go with the group. Ian has become positively antisocial lately. It's almost as if he really enjoys being an outcast.

As for me, I enjoyed being part of the group. I liked having somebody to talk to about clothes and Eddie and what kind of eyeliner to buy and all the other stuff that we never talk about at home. I liked being able to sit at Shelley's house and watch videos with stereophonic sound. Maybe Shelley and Debbie and the others weren't intellectual superstars, as Ian kept pointing out. Maybe they didn't care about saving the whales or preserving the ozone layer. Maybe they didn't really understand everything I had to say, or thought I was clowning around when I told them that aerosol hair spray was killing the atmosphere. So what? At least they were normal. At least they gave me a chance to talk about normal girl things like makeup and music and boys. I'm sixteen years old and think I deserve a little bit of normality in my life.

What I didn't deserve was going to the airport in Margaret's ancient Honda. Shelley and Debbie were leaving for Mexico the same afternoon, and I was afraid they might get to the airport early and see us. Thank God they didn't. Margaret was wearing some sack of a dress that looked like it had been made from a rice bag, the kind of outfit that made her deserve a nickname like Vulgaris. Rick was in a kind of Indian suit, the sort of thing that went out with Gandhi. And Ian was Ian.

The four of us at the airport made one very strange, awkward group. I was wearing a new skirt and blouse, a set I had picked out with Debbie, and was looking very adult. I stood next to Ian, who was dressed like a poster child for Save the Children. On the other side of the metal detectors stood Rick and Margaret, looking like they'd just left Woodstock. I shook my head and waved good-bye. Rick replied with a peace sign. Margaret just smiled, something she shouldn't do until she gets her teeth fixed.

I tried to put my arm around Ian to bring him along to the gate.

"I can move without your assistance," he said, shrugging off my arm. "You're not my mother, you know."

I resolved right then to pay no attention to him on the flight.

Ian has been in a perpetually bad mood lately, which has something to do with school and a kid called Missing Link and the fact that Ian is so obnoxious anyway. He seems to spend all his time these days hiding out at the university or making these funny maps and diagrams. Maybe he's finally cracked, like my father.

I left Ian at the back of the plane and took a seat next to an advertising executive who looked *very* California: blond hair, designer shirt and tie, perfect smile. He talked to me about how much he hated flying but had to do it anyway and how nice I looked and where was I going and could he buy me a drink. The guy was older than Rick, but I still enjoyed the attention. After all, Eddie was a nice guy, but he wasn't the only guy in the world.

The ad executive gave me his card when I left the plane, saying I should give him a call. I smiled and said thanks, though I figured that he was still a bit beyond me. I had too much else on my mind, anyhow.

Somewhere in the crowd of people waiting with their noses pressed to the waiting room window was my mother. I scanned the crowd while I stood with Ian as the luggage came spewing out of the plane, but there was nobody I recognized out there.

At last my suitcases appeared, then Ian's duffel bag. We hauled the three pieces through the last security check, then made our way into the crowd. I kept looking into the crush of smiling faces. Where was she? Had she screwed this whole thing up, right at the very end?

"Libby," I heard. "Ian."

I couldn't see where the voice had come from, so I just stood still. Then I felt two arms around me and kisses all over my face.

It was her! I could hardly believe it. There was my mother, standing right in front of me, dressed in a blue business suit and Gucci shoes. My mother!

"You see, Libby," she said, hugging Ian. "Everything has changed. For the better."

I guess it had. Here was my mother, all dressed up and looking . . . well, successful. Even the last picture she had sent didn't give me any idea she'd be like this.

"Come on, both of you. I want you to meet Michael."

She grabbed one of my suitcases, took Ian by the hand, and led us outside the crowd. Standing there was a man who could have been a clone of the guy on the plane: blond, well-dressed, handsome, and smiling. How did my mother ever land him?

"This is Michael," my mother said proudly. "The man who straightened out my life."

"Well, the first part is right," Michael said to us, smiling. "Did you two have a good flight?"

"Great," I said, still sort of dazed.

"It was acceptable," Ian said, in that snotty, formal way he talks sometimes.

"Well, we're both glad you could be here," Michael replied.

I felt like I was stepping into some sort of dream world. Oh, I talked about the plane and sensible things like that, but that was just a cover. What really mattered was what I couldn't believe — my mother, this man, California.

We left the airline terminal and took a people mover to their car, a silver Mercedes. Michael put our luggage in the trunk, took off his suit jacket and laid it on top, then unlocked all the doors of the car with one turn of the key.

"Why don't you two women climb in the back, and Ian and I can take the front," Michael suggested.

That sounded good, especially the "women" part of it, so I climbed in beside my mother. Ian got into the front seat, obviously still in a cruddy mood. I don't think he'd smiled once since we got off the plane.

"I want the two of you to see the city as we go into it," my mom said. "San Francisco has got to be the most beautiful place in the world. And for the next two weeks, it's all yours. I'm taking some time off work and I want to show you everything."

We drove into the city on the freeway, ending up right downtown. Michael pointed out his law office somewhere in the stratosphere of the Transamerica building. Then we drove by the television station where my mother worked. Finally we went out along Mission Street, then up and down some hills that justified cable cars. The city was glowing in the sunshine, just like I was glowing inside.

After this quick tour, Michael took the Mercedes up a street so steep that I knew Margaret's old Honda would never have made it. At the top, we pulled into a parking space bricked out in front of an old Victorian town house. The place was from another century, all curlicued and stained-glassed.

"Home," my mother said.

"It's wild," I said.

"Wait till you see the inside."

The inside. If the outside was like the last century, the inside was like the next. Everything was new, with big windows in the back that let sunlight pour into the place. The furniture, the walls, the lights — everything was so clean, so modern. I put down my suitcases and walked into the living space, an area twice as large as the house I'd left that morning.

"The back of the house is all new," Michael was explaining to Ian. "The previous owners kept the facade, but gutted everything else and rebuilt. It took me two weeks to figure out how to get the Jacuzzi to work."

Michael smiled. Ian did not. Maybe he was overwhelmed. This place was the kind of thing I'd seen in magazines at Shelley's house. It was probably way beyond anything Ian could even imagine.

Our two weeks in California went zooming by faster than I could believe. I remember a few details: a foggy day on Fisherman's Wharf before lunch; driving over the Golden Gate Bridge to Muir Woods; a pre-Broadway musical; my mom's television studio; a wonderful party; and a guy named Mark.

Mark and the party should probably be joined together on my list. I met him just before New Year's. The get-together was arranged by one of the partners in Michael's law firm. Mark was the son of still another partner, and he seemed all California: curly bleached hair, muscles that rippled under his shirt, teeth too white to be real. We started off just talking, but by the end of the evening he had his arm around me, pointing out sights in the city's dark night. It was wonderful, but of course nothing could really happen. I wasn't from California, was I? And I had to go back home, didn't I?

In the real world, I had to fly back in two more days. I was miserable, of course, even after sleeping until noon. I spent the afternoon putting stuff in suitcases, packing up the new clothes my mom had bought for me. Just to make my mood worse, Ian was smiling for the first time since we arrived.

I was glad when Michael offered to take Ian out that night to some weird play at a theater near Berkeley. I was sick of his stupid grin. Besides, it gave me a chance to stay home with Mom and finish getting ready for the trip.

"I'm making some coffee, Libby," my mom said. "You want a cup?"

"Yeah," I told her, snapping my suitcases closed. "I'll be down."

My mother had the coffee maker going when I came downstairs. The hot tub bubbled away, not far from the Christmas tree, and the big back windows were covered in mist.

"How do you feel about going back?" Mom asked, sitting beside me. Her voice seemed to catch in the middle of the question.

"I don't know," I said.

"Well, are you getting on okay now?"

"Better than before. I've got those friends I told you about. The only real problem is Rick and Ian, really. They sort of drive me crazy." I laughed, just a little.

"Your father never grows up, does he?" she said with the hint of a smile.

"Well, the bookstore is changing. Since they wrecked the Albania display, he's thinking about fixing the place up. Or maybe he's just waiting for a new shipment of Wonderful Albania posters."

"Sounds like your father. I think Granny Mc-Naughton protects him from the real world. He's never had to really face anything, not the way I have. You have to learn to make compromises. And then you can do all right for yourself."

I looked around the room and let my mother's point sink in.

"After I left," she went on, "I spent a lot of time just growing up. Your father and I, we were from some other time. Throwbacks to some crazy age of drugs and beads and funny ideas about the world." She stopped and smiled. "But all of that was just impossible to keep going — that's what I found out. After the rabbits and the health food store and the bust, well, it was just too much. It took me a long time to figure out why. I had to look at me. Look hard at who I was."

"Is that what you were doing all that time?"

"I guess," my mom said. "I had to put myself back together in some way that made sense. Rick and I lived in never-never land, not wanting to grow up. But you know, Libby, there isn't any pixie dust. Sooner or later you've got to come back and make it right here, in the real world." She looked out the window at the lights sparkling on the next hill. "It took me three years to figure that out. Getting my head together — that's what we used to call it."

"But why'd you have to leave?" I asked. Maybe that was the real question all along.

"Because I couldn't do anything back there. Everything was falling apart — the store, the drugs, the big dream — and I was falling apart, too. You kids couldn't see it, but I knew. There was Rick with his crazy ideas of liberating Elmira. And Granny always backing him up. And there was me, sitting with a couple of years of college education, doing nothing but looking after two little kids. No, make that three little kids. I began to feel that my whole life was in a box that was getting smaller, day after day. That's when I knew. I realized I was destroying myself, killing whatever potential I had. Somehow I had to get away so I could come back a real human being."

The room was quiet except for the humming and bubbling of the hot tub.

"You couldn't do it there?" I said. I guess I was challenging her, I don't know. Somehow it came out sounding like Ian.

"No. I tried — you have no idea how hard I tried. Night school classes and correspondence courses and anything, anything to break free. But I couldn't do it, not then," she said, looking at me. "Libby, you must be able to understand how hard it is to grow in that kind of environment. I mean, you're living with Rick now, trying to change yourself. Your new friends, your clothes, everything. But Rick is always there, half crazy —"

"He's not that bad. Ian is worse," I said.

"Still, you can feel the way they hold you back. I had to break free of that."

"By yourself?"

"Oh, Libby. You think it was easy just leaving you two behind? You were my babies . . ." Her words died out. "But I wanted to do what was best for you. I knew that Rick and Mrs. McNaughton could look after you and, for a while, I didn't have any idea what I was going to do. It was all so confused. After I left, I felt so awful for so long, like there was an empty place inside me . . ."

I wanted to say something, but my eyes were misting up and my throat felt dry.

"Libby, I'm so sorry," my mom said, putting her

arm around me. "I know I can never make that up to you, the hurt. Nothing can make that up. But I want to try. We have this big house. We can give you everything."

"You mean, live here?" I asked. I'd thought about it, dreamed about it already, with all sorts of mixed feelings.

"When you're ready," my mom said. "It's here for both of you. Soon you'll be ready for college. Why not San Jose? Or sooner. This fall, if you want to finish high school here."

"But what about Rick?"

"What about *you*, Libby? What kind of life do you deserve to live?"

I looked up and saw that her eyes were rimmed with tears. I knew how she felt.

"Oh, Mom," I said, throwing my arms around her.

We were both crying now. "There's so much here for you, Libby. But I don't want to push you . . . Oh, I don't know what to say. I just want you to know that I'm here, and that I want you with me, and . . . I love you."

I felt so confused. I'd blamed my mom for so long for leaving us when we needed her. But now she was back in my life, not just a voice on the phone or a hurried letter from almost three thousand miles away, but right beside me. Wanting me with her.

That night, for me, it meant everything.

12

· · · · · · · ·

Ian

I knew from the start that Sharon wanted more than just vacation time with the kids. At the very least, she wanted us to see a transformation: our new, improved mother, now with poverty-fighting disposable cash, as the announcer might say. I was supposed to be impressed.

It began with the envelope the tickets arrived in — stationery from where Sharon worked, typed. I ought to have known that something was up. Sharon couldn't type; her fingers and hands are as crooked and unruly as mine. That meant she had a secretary. And *that* meant she had some position of responsibility.

Responsibility? It's hard to use the word in connection with Sharon, a lady whose concept of responsibility seemed to disappear when the going got tough five years ago. Maybe she had fooled some people out there, at least this lawyer Michael and maybe a few people at the television station. But she couldn't fool me.

So why did I go, an earthling might ask. I was busy

enough formulating a scheme to use against Missing Link, playing Dungeons & Dragons with R.T., and working with Rick at the bookstore. I had every reason to stay. Yet any suggestion I made to that effect was looked upon as insanity by both Rick and Libby. Of course I was going. In fact, nobody even asked me after the first night. They just assumed that I'd be flying off to Yuppieland in December, that I really wanted to spend Christmas with elevator music and palm trees.

So rather than make a big deal about it, I went. I had a hunch there was something capital-I Impressive that I was supposed to see in California, so why not see it and get the thing over with?

There they were: Mother, Boyfriend, Car, House. My Mother had apparently burned all her denim outfits, loaded up with dresses from the Gucci warehouse, and rebuilt her life to fit. Her Boyfriend, Michael, might have come from the same warehouse. He was just what one would expect of a California attorney — blond, trendy, rich — only he wasn't an airhead. In fact, he was very smart for an earthling, probably quite out of place in California. Sometimes I wondered why he got involved with Sharon.

The Car was a Simonized baby Mercedes. It was one of those cars that made all sorts of statements, like "I'm expensive but sporty." Inside it had white leather upholstery that made the seats look like German sausage.

And then the House. Earthlings began some ages ago in caves, made it up to mud huts over a million years, took another hundred thousand to tame mud into brick and branches into planks. Then it took only a thousand years until earthlings could build the kind of house Granny owned: sensible, simple shelter that kept one dry in summer and warm in winter. That's what an earthling house is all about.

But not Michael and Sharon's house. That house had about as much to do with shelter as the Mercedes had to do with my father's bicycle. That house was designed by somebody who had seen one James Bond movie too many. I kept expecting beds to come shooting out of the wall or hidden tables to come up from the floor. Michael even admitted it had taken him two weeks to learn how to operate the bathtub. The bathtub!

"Ian, cut it out," Libby whispered to me that first night.

"Cut what out? What's 'it'?"

"The way you're acting. Everybody is trying so hard to be nice and you're always in a lousy mood."

"People shouldn't have to try so hard," I told her. "And I'm only acting this way because I feel underdressed just standing in the living room."

"See, there you go again. Now stop it and give them a chance, will you?"

Well, I tried. I wasn't kidding about being underdressed. The house was the kind of place where even your pajamas ought to have a designer label. And I didn't even own pajamas.

I managed to be civil all through breakfast. I was charming when I met the housekeeper. I asked perky questions as we drove through the city and down to my mother's office. I acted suitably impressed by the TV studio, by lunch, by dinner at the Wharf. The only time I became the least bit obnoxious was when

Sharon wanted to buy me some clothes. It seemed to me at the time that my jeans, boots, and T-shirts were plenty good enough for any kind of New Year's party I would like to attend. But Libby shot me one of her more despairing looks, and I gave in. To be nice.

My mother had organized almost all our waking minutes in California. She had to work two days out of the two weeks, but even on those days we had a suggested itinerary. I found all this organization hard to take. Maybe since she was a scheduling manager at the station it made sense, but it was still wearing me out. By the party on New Year's Eve, all I really wanted to do was curl up with one of the books I'd brought with me.

Instead, I had to get dressed up in some clothes that were too scratchy, too tight, and too colorful for any self-respecting alien. Then I had to walk through the fog to a place three blocks down that seemed to be a clone of Michael's house. And then I had to be pleasant. People kept on talking about "the East," as if any place where it snowed at Christmas had to be ever so quaint. I had to fight to keep my mouth shut. Be nice, they're only earthlings, I kept telling myself.

I think my mother had the party organized along with everything else. I noticed that Libby very quickly got going with some blond and curly surfer. Of course, Libby has a failing for these athletic types, perhaps because she has recently abandoned her own natural string bean physique. But it occurred to me that this might be her real milieu, the place where Libby belonged. Maybe this was the kind of life all earthlings really wanted to live.

There was also a girl for me at the party, or at least

an earthling of my age. She lacked the large breasts we aliens prefer, but was otherwise about as close to an earthling dream teenager as anything I've ever seen in the flesh. I will confess that she was attractive even to me — until I talked to her.

"Hi," she said.

"Hi," I said. Propitious start. Her eyes were extraordinarily blue; I attributed this to the climate.

"Fly in?" she asked.

"Beamed down," I said.

"You're funny."

"Funny strange?"

"Funny ha-ha," she said, smiling perfectly.

It occurred to me that we had fallen into a California speech pattern — two-word sentences. I thought I might test out deeper waters.

"I'm reading Piers Anthony," I said. "What are people reading out here?"

"We watch videos," she said, still smiling.

"Oh. Well, what's it like to live in the lap of luxury like this? There's enough wealth on this block to feed most of Africa for years."

"It's boring."

"Oh," I said again. I suppose anything can be boring if you really work at it.

"You bring dope?" she asked.

"Uh, no."

"Too bad," she said, her blue-blue eyes looking around the room.

She seemed to be losing interest fast, so I tried to give our limping conversation another chance to get up and run.

"We went to Muir Woods last week to see those

amazing trees," I began. "I suppose you get to go there any time you want."

"I went, once."

"Well, the great thing is that the forest has been protected," I said. "So many of the forests near us are in trouble from the way development keeps pushing in on them. Of course there's the Sierra Club —"

"Is that like Parachute Club?" she asked, dreamily.

I was stunned. "Uh, no."

"Too bad." She sighed. "I like their videos." Then her blue-blue eyes found someone on the other side of the room and she began floating away from me.

I didn't follow her. I stood there, in that over-crowded, overdressed, overmonied living room, and wondered just how someone could grow up so physically perfect and so mentally undernourished.

On the last day, Michael offered to take us all to the theater, but Sharon and Libby said no. So he took me, which might be what he had in mind all along. We went to this little theater up near Berkeley that was doing two strange plays by a playwright named Beckett. Not the sort of entertainment to appeal to either Libby or Sharon, who were ecstatic over a tacky musical we saw during Christmas week, but more my kind of cerebral material.

I liked the theater immediately. It was a converted garage, the kind of place where one might see a hydraulic lift in the stage area. The inside was a mess of hard seats, light tracks, leftover sets from other plays, and a pile of sand. Some of the people in the audience wore suits and ties, but a lot of them wore jeans and grungy shirts. I felt at home.

But I wasn't quite so sure what to make of the plays.

The first one was a short mime play where one actor kept getting thrown back on stage from the wings. Things came down from the ceiling to tempt him, but they never seemed to be within his reach. I kept thinking that the whole thing was a metaphor for my father's life — idealistic but frustrated.

The second play was a long one called *Endgame* and it had dialogue, but strange dialogue. Michael said it was translated from the French. I said, "Oh." I couldn't figure out what it was supposed to be about, but Michael said it had something to do with *Hamlet,* one of those plays I've always been meaning to read.

When the plays were finished, Michael took me out for coffee and dessert at one of the places downtown that offer forty-two different kinds of cake at four bucks a slice. The deal seemed too good to turn down. Even aliens have a sweet tooth.

By the time the desserts actually arrived, we had talked out the plays and were moving into the central material of the evening. The pitch. The one I'd been expecting all along.

"Have you had a good time out here?" Michael asked me.

"Good enough," I said.

"Life here is different from back home. We're busy and relaxed simultaneously. I remember when I moved out here after Columbia I had a hard time getting used to it. Real culture shock."

"I guess I've been feeling that," I told him.

"It's been easier for Libby, I suppose, to deal with some of the changes. She seems to like it out here and get on pretty well."

"Seems to."

"And what about you?" he asked. I didn't know if this was idle talk or serious cross-examination. "You seemed pretty hostile at first, but now I don't know what you think."

"Well, I'm not really at home anyplace," I explained.

"Still waiting for the mother ship to beam you up?" he asked. He was smiling at me.

"Libby told you."

"So did you," he said. "But the real question is, what do you do if there's no mother ship? What if all there is — is just what you see?"

"Then you try to make things work a little better," I told him. "Maybe you set up a window display on Albania —"

"That's what I used to think," Michael broke in. "I used to think that somehow you could make the system work. Make a utopia right here. After all, who wants to live in anything less? But after knocking my head against reality a few times, I've decided that the system is a lot bigger and stronger than I am. Maybe instead of rebuilding it all you can do is give it a nudge in the right direction."

I kept picturing my father, like the guy in the play, running full tilt and then falling flat on his face.

"So you put on your three-piece suit and spend your days nudging, eh?" I asked him.

"I guess I've made some compromises to get where I am," he said. "And you resent it, don't you?"

"Yeah," I said, staring back at him. It was the only honest connection we'd made in two weeks.

"You think there's something morally superior about living in a shack and wondering where next week's food is going to come from or if the cops are going to shut down the store?"

"Maybe."

"Well, I've been there, Ian, and that's not moral superiority. That's a kind of slavery. It's a way to retreat from the world into a crazy kind of personal moral utopia. It's not real. Real is having time not to worry about staying alive, and having the clout to do something when you can."

"When you can — or when it's convenient?" I said, arching one eyebrow. "And how does that massive Jacuzzi tub fit into your wonderful moral universe?"

Michael smiled and began an answer as slippery as if it were greased with suntan lotion. I kept accusing and he kept justifying, but in the end we had gotten nowhere — except that I was ready to be beamed up.

"Let's go," I said. "The plane leaves pretty early."

"And you definitely want to be on it?" Michael asked.

"Sure I do. Why wouldn't I?"

"I'm not sure Libby is that happy about going back. And she doesn't have to. Neither do you."

"What's all this?" I said. Though I knew. I knew the pitch was coming. I had a hunch that Libby and I were supposed to become their new toys, now that they were bored with the Jacuzzi and the Mercedes.

"Your mother would love to have both of you live with us, not just come for visits. So would I, Ian, though you may not want to believe that. I think we could probably work something out with your father."

"Probably. But you'd have a harder time working it out with me."

"You're right," he said, pulling out a credit card to

pay the bill. "You've got to look at the two sides of it yourself. Maybe you feel one way now, but you might feel a different way in a year or two. All I can say is that the offer is there, whenever you want to take it."

I looked up and saw that Michael was neither smiling nor frowning. He wasn't much of a salesman, really, arguing too much with the customer to be very convincing. Maybe he knew all along that I was going to say no, that I'd always tell him no.

But Libby? That made me wonder.

13

· · · · · · · · · ·

Libby

Flying back on the plane was like waking up from a wonderful dream only to find that the guy you're hugging is really a pillow and that your feet are sticking out from under the blanket. You end up feeling a little foolish and a lot cold. I guess I knew I had to go home, even if only to finish up the school year, but that didn't mean I wanted to. Any more than I wanted to sit next to Ian on the plane. But the flight was so crowded, I didn't have any choice.

I hoped that Ian might get some headphones and listen to music on the flight, but he told the stewardess no, mumbling something about twelve varieties of elevator music. I fished out a *Cosmopolitan* magazine I'd bought at the newsstand before we left and hoped for silence. Fat chance.

"Did you get the pitch last night?" Ian asked me when I had just settled down.

"What pitch?"

"The sales job. Come and join us in sunny California — isn't that how the jingle goes?" Ian said in his usual cynical voice.

"I had a long talk with Mom, if that's what you mean," I told him, putting the magazine on my lap. "She said we both could come and live with them if we wanted. Is that what you call a pitch?"

"Libby, the whole thing was a pitch," Ian began. "Two weeks in California, all expenses paid. It's like the kind of thing you win on 'The Price Is Right,' except we didn't have to guess the cost. The whole thing is a sales job, advertising, another way to con the consumer."

"Ian, do I have to listen to this for the next four hours?" He was starting on one of those pompous little lectures I find so boring.

"I just want to know what happened to you," he said, cutting the lecture off.

"We had some coffee. We talked. Mom said there was lots of room in the house and that they'd love to have us. We talked about my going to San Jose State. That's about all."

"You didn't promise anything?" Ian asked. He seemed really upset, as if what I did made some big difference to him.

"Not yet, no," I told him. "I'm not going to say anything for you, anyhow. Did Michael talk to you about it?"

"He tried, but I wasn't too receptive," Ian said.

"Well, bully for you."

I brought my magazine back up and looked through the *Cosmo* quiz. It was twenty questions to determine the inner you. Question one went, If you could bring only one thing with you on a safari, would it be (a) Michael J. Fox, (b) a book, (c) a portable stereo, (d) makeup. I debated between (a) and (c), then marked

(d) on the answer sheet because I knew Ian was watching me.

"I figured." Ian sniffed as he looked at my answer.

"It's just a joke, Ian. Your trouble is that you take life so seriously that you can't have fun."

"I do have fun," he replied.

"Like what? Reading some stupid science-fiction novel? Seeing how often that kid at school can beat you up?" I asked him.

"Nobody's beat me up in months," he said.

"That's just because the kid broke his leg. Wait till the cast comes off and he gets back in form. Besides, I think you like the attention. You're a masochist."

"Wow, big word, Libby. I bet you didn't use anything like that in California — you'd have to explain it to them."

"Michael is probably brighter than you are, Ian," I said flatly.

"He's probably brighter than all of us." Ian grunted. "I have to give him credit — he figured out that society would pay him a lot more for cheating old ladies out of insurance claims against Safeway than it would for defending guys who need legal aid. His math is impeccable, probably a hundred times better than my math. But look where the money comes from."

"Why should I?" I shot back, putting the magazine down again. "You think we're so wonderful because we haven't got two cents to rub together? Or because Rick pushes books on Albania instead of best-sellers? Grow up, Ian."

"At least I don't have to suck up to insurance companies or give phony smiles to the jerky passengers on a plane just to make a buck," Ian said as a stewardess passed by.

"What's the matter? Losing your big vocabulary when somebody challenges you?"

Ian frowned at me and corrected himself. "It's an existential question — who are you or what are you? Michael has all the nice liberal phrases down, he gives to all the right causes, but his nine to five is being a legal hit man. And that's what buys the big house, the big car, even the clothes you're wearing."

"The clothes we're both wearing," I corrected him, staring at the shirt my mom had bought a week before.

"At least I didn't ask for it," he shot back.

"And I did," I told him. "So what? I happen to like decent clothes and a car that doesn't break down and a house that doesn't always smell like ginger and fried rice. I happen to like the makeup on my face and guys who don't have zits and a show that's going to open on Broadway in two weeks. So what?"

"You didn't used to be like that," Ian muttered.

"That's right. I used to be an ugly, skinny kid who shot off her mouth in class and got beat up in the playground. I used to go around wearing Salvation Army sacks, telling everybody that I wouldn't wear their nice clothes even if somebody paid me. I used to walk around with my nose stuck up in the air when all the time I had my feet, my everything, stuck in the gutter."

"Bravo," Ian said. "A brilliant speech, Libby. But I've got a better question."

"Yeah?"

"What are you now?"

He looked at me like a little troll, his big eyes

bulging out, a stupid grin on his face. I closed my magazine and unfastened my seat belt. Someplace on a plane of this size there had to be an empty seat, and I went to find it.

Rick and Margaret came to the airport to pick us up, dressed in exactly the same outfits they wore to drop us off. My father looked stranger than ever, his deep-set eyes always focused on some vague infinity that nobody else could see. He and Margaret held hands like two aging orphans lost in the big world of the airport.

Needless to say, I wasn't in a splendid mood. And things went downhill when I saw Shelley's parents at the far end of the airport waiting to pick up Debbie and her. I hid my face so they wouldn't see me with Rick and Vulgaris, then almost had to push my father out the door to the parking lot.

We got back to the little house that Granny had given us and I carried my luggage in through the slush. Talk about depressing. After California, our house looked smaller and dumpier than ever. My father had bought a new sack of rice that was taking up most of the kitchen, like a squatting Buddha. The smell of cooking vegetables and incense was almost over-powering.

I left everything downstairs, went to my room, and threw myself on the bed. Why had I come back? What kind of life did I have here?

The telephone rang and somebody answered it. Then I heard Ian shouting upstairs, "Libby, it's for you."

"Who is it?" I yelled back. I didn't feel like talking to anybody.

"Rabbit."

"Tell her I'm taking a nap. Tell her I'm sick." Both of those were almost true — maybe not physically true, but truthful in another way. I just felt like I was only half alive. And I'd only been back for an hour. How would I ever survive a week?

I lay on the bed for a long time, thinking about my mother and Michael and the two weeks with them. It was all such a blur, all filled with color and life and everything we didn't have here. I looked around my own bedroom, the walls I had painted myself, the prints I had bought at Applebee's, the lousy little desk I still hadn't repainted, the piles of old clothes on the floor that I'd never wear again. Then I thought back to the room in California, the nice white walls, the lights set into the ceiling, the big framed posters of Magritte and Calder, the clean pine furniture.

The phone rang again.

"Libby?" Ian called up. "You want to take this one?" he said. He must have felt like some sort of secretary.

"Who is it?"

"Some snob."

"Cut the editorial. Who is it?"

"Shelley Patterson, I think, but all your pretentious friends sound pretty much the same."

"I'll take it," I told him, swinging myself out of bed.

When I got downstairs, the phone was buried under a beanbag chair. Ian's idea of a little joke.

I dug it out. "Shelley?" I asked.

"Shelley the Sunburned," she said. "I got so burned the first day I could barely move from the suite. How'd your visit go?"

"Oh, Shelley, it was so fabulous I just can't believe it . . ."

14

. . . .

Ian

Disneyland isn't just *in* California; Disneyland *is* California. That's what Libby can't understand.

Now I have nothing against a good fantasy. But there are times and places for them — like lying in your bed at night, or sitting in English while Mrs. Proctor reads a poem, or when observing Marci Macdonald in a tight sweater. There should not be a whole state devoted to fantasy.

The people in California — and I had better limit this to upper-middle-class white people in California — have nothing to do with real life. Michael spends his time trying to keep mythical insurance companies from paying astronomical sums of money to people with purely imaginary injuries. Sharon makes money by selling time — imagine that! — selling time on some middle-wave frequencies that carry programs based on impossible people in impossible situations. In order to see reality, they buy tickets to a play that turns out to be a pre-Broadway musical. Do people sing and dance their way through real life?

No, for most of us it's a case of eat, sleep, and try to leave some kind of chalk mark on life.

Libby was the one who got addicted to the fantasy. It was like a daily injection for two weeks, and she was hooked. No wonder she was so upset when she had to leave. From the moment she got on the plane to go home, she was like a junkie going cold turkey. I expected to see tremens and a cold sweat on her upper lip. How could I tell her that the California fantasy was just one more dream, like her snobby friends and her cosmetic face — and that sooner or later we all have to wake up?

Needless to say, I was quite happy to be home. I like the fact that Rick and Vulgaris have only a couple sets of clothes to wear. It seems to me that anybody who can wear a different suit every day for two weeks has got to have his values too firmly set on appearances. Rick did not land any big accounts or win any cases or sell any prime-time shows over the two weeks — he bought a big sack of rice. Now *that* is reality.

As soon as I got back to the house, I phoned R.T. to see if my own alien reality was in any great danger. He lived just down the street from Missing Link, so he could give me an update on the state of his leg.

"How was it?" he asked me almost as soon as he picked up the phone.

"A fairy tale."

"Did you get to Disneyland?" he asked.

"All the time," I told him, but he couldn't possibly have known what I meant. "Look, what about Missing Link?"

"He's still a cripple."

"The full cast has got to be off by now."

"Yeah, but he must have something else on his leg. Maybe there were complications. Falling down stairs is one thing, but getting stomped over by two other guys could have given him a multiple fracture. Anyway, we still have some time. Have you got the plan worked out?"

"Almost," I told him. "I've got most of the tunnels mapped out."

"Then what?"

"Then I'll explain it to you. The less you know now, the better," I said.

One thing I like about R.T. is that he'll accept a line like that, the kind of thing you'd use in a spy film, and not question it. The world needs more people like R.T. It probably needs fewer of me.

Beam me up before I hurt somebody, will you?

At dinner that night, Rick looked up from his snow peas with a funny smile on his face. "Do you think the two of you could come down to the store tonight?"

"I'm going to Shelley's," Libby announced.

"No, I'd like you to come to the store," Rick said. His deep voice was a little louder than usual.

Libby looked up from her greasy hamburger. I think she was a little surprised that Rick had disagreed with her.

"Well, I made arrangements," she said.

"And I would really like you to come with me," Rick countered.

I was enjoying this. Rick doesn't usually get involved with what he calls a power trip, but obviously our going with him was important for some reason not yet clear to us.

"Da-ad," Libby whined.

"Come on, Libby," I butted in. "It's not as if going

to Shelley's were the same as dinner at the White House."

Rick just stared at Libby. His look conveyed some combination of anger and hurt, though the proportions weren't clear to me.

"Okay, but I've got to call her first."

"No problem," Rick answered, and the tension dissolved.

Libby spent something like half an hour on the phone while the two of us cludded around the house in our boots. Then she yelled out the question "Do I have to work?"

"No," Rick said, then added, "Why?"

"I'm just trying to decide what to wear."

I exchanged a look with my father, then pressed an imaginary ice cream cone into my forehead. Could this be the same sister who built half the shelves at Rick's old health food store?

Half an hour later, the three of us headed off. Rick and I looked vaguely like lumberjacks, Libby like some fashion model who'd gotten lost in a Monty Python sketch. The bookstore is only five blocks from the house, but from all Libby's complaining you'd think asking her to do that much walking was like asking her to cross the Arctic on foot. Basically, she was annoyed at having to spend time with us. Basically, *I* was annoyed at having her along.

Rick simply said nothing.

When we reached the store, I understood immediately what Rick wanted to show us — a transformation.

In the window was a neon sign that glowed RICK'S BOOKROOM. The old painted sign up above had been redone with the same logo.

"Impressive," I said.

"Pretty slick," Libby said. I wasn't sure if she was being appreciative or snotty.

"I know this man who's into neon," Rick explained. "He convinced me that I needed a new sign and a new logo, so I put some of the renovation money into that."

"Renovation money?" Libby asked.

"From Granny," Rick replied. Then he unlocked the front door and took us inside. A flip of the light switch showed us another change.

"Floodlights on the window display," I said.

"The neon man was really into light, and they had these floods down at the Salvation Army," Rick explained.

I had to smile. It was the mix, the modern lights and the Salvation Army source, that still showed Rick's touch.

Then I looked around the store. The place was entirely rebuilt — nice painted shelves, revolving racks, a wall of paperbacks, a bunch of best-sellers at the front. This may not seem too extraordinary for the average bookstore, but Rick had never run an average bookstore; he ran a "propaganda shop," as Libby put it. In two weeks, he had yanked the propaganda out and turned the place into a highbrow Waldenbooks.

"Look at this," Libby said, pointing at the rack in front of the still-ancient cash register, "Judith Krantz? What's all this junk for?" she asked.

"It's bait," Rick said.

"Bait?"

"It's going to lure the masses in," Rick explained. "I began thinking that maybe a hundred and twenty-eight customers a week wasn't enough. I had the dead weeks after Christmas to work, a little money, a lot of friends to help. This is the result."

He had a look on his face like a father with a newborn baby. But there was also something that seemed to ask approval, as if he wasn't really sure that he had done the right thing.

"It's great," I told him. "You'll double your customers in no time."

Libby said nothing. She seemed to be looking around almost critically. Something like this ought to be just what she wanted, almost like California, but she didn't seem too happy with it.

"What happened to Albania?" was all she said.

"I split up the new books," Rick explained. "I've got some in travel, some in philosophy, some in political science. And there's still a poster."

He pointed to one wall so we'd notice it, and there it was: Beautiful Albania. But the poster was framed now, and looked like the kind of travel poster you'd see for Greece or Bermuda. It wasn't shouting "Commie Paradise!" anymore; it was doing a real soft sell.

Libby walked past the paperback shelves to a new magazine rack at the back. She stopped there and looked it over, bending down to pick up a thick magazine.

"Architectural Digest?" she asked.

"For the yuppies," Rick said. He seemed embarrassed, trying to justify all this. "But there's a real assortment — new wave magazines from Paris, women's liberation stuff from New York, art mags, underground mags, you name it."

"I can see," Libby said, picking up a tabloid called *Gay Today.*

108

"How do people like it?" I asked Rick.

"I don't know yet. We're going to reopen tomorrow. I've got some ads going on the radio to announce it," he said.

"Advertising? You?" Libby asked, staring at him.

"Well, the man who was into neon —"

"— was also into advertising," Libby concluded for him. She shook her head and wandered around the store, looking at everything like she was checking the place for dust or health violations.

"Well, at the risk of repeating myself," I said, "I'm impressed. This is the kind of thing you should have done years ago. Now if you got yourself a computer and set up a decent accounting system, this might be a real business."

"I was thinking about that," Rick said simply.

"I can't believe what's going on," Libby told us, but she wasn't smiling. It wasn't the way she used "fabulous" to describe California or "I can't believe it" when my mother said she was taking us to a musical. It was some other kind of disbelief.

"Can't believe what?" I asked her.

"That you really want a store like this."

"Why wouldn't I?" Rick asked her.

"Because it's not *you*," she said, as if the *you* explained everything. As if her own *you* hadn't rotated a hundred eighty degrees in the last year.

I shook my head and tried to exchange a look with Rick. But he wouldn't look at me. He wouldn't look at Libby, either. He was staring way off, the way he did when he meditated, but his face didn't look peaceful. It looked hurt.

15

Libby

I should have known that the new bookstore would bring its own disaster. Rick's Bookroom was too commercial, too sensible, too *successful* to be connected with my father. Of course, Ian would argue that the new store was blessed with my father's quirky interests — fantasy novels and yoga and fringe magazines and books on every cause known to man. But I just couldn't imagine that this was really *Rick's* bookroom, as the neon sign said. Not unless my father, like me, was somehow changing his life.

Of course, I said nothing. I was sure, somewhere deep down, that the bookstore was doomed like everything else in my father's life: like his marriage, his rabbit farm, his health food store. And I didn't have to wait long for that doom to strike.

I was at Shelley's house when the phone call came. We were watching some videos on the big projection TV, sipping some Cokes in frosted glasses. When the phone rang, Shelley answered it and then handed it to me.

"It's for you," she said. "Somebody from another solar system." She smiled and the others laughed. I had made Ian's Moonkid fantasy a kind of standing joke in the group, sort of like Debbie's crazy uncle who started hang gliding after hearing the voice of God while watching the Johnny Carson show. Except I made Ian sound even weirder than that. It was one of the ways I got the group to accept me — as much as they *ever* accepted me.

I took the portable phone from Debbie's hand and began walking away from the others. I had a hunch that Ian was calling about some kind of disaster, so I figured it might be best to get someplace where the others couldn't hear me.

"Ian, why are you calling me *here?*" I whispered.

"Because that's where you are," he shot back at me. "Besides, it's important, Lib."

"What's important?"

"The bookstore's been busted," Ian said. "They've taken Rick to the jail."

I was stunned. I'd been expecting some disaster, but not so soon, and not like this. I had a sudden flashback to the drug bust in Elmira, sitting up in bed, the voices of my father and strange men — the police — in the store down below. For just a second, I felt that terror again.

"Libby, did you hear me?" Ian asked.

"I heard you," I said, snapping out of it. By then I had walked the phone upstairs to the library, where no one else could listen in. "What was it for this time? Possession?"

"It's not that kind of bust. They're charging him with selling pornography."

"Ian, if this is some kind of joke — "

"I'm not kidding," he said. "Rick just called from the holding center. Granny's calling her lawyer to arrange bail, and I'm going down to the jail to be with him. I could get the taxi to stop off and pick you up."

"No, no," I said. I felt so afraid, for all of us. "Don't come here — it would be too hard to explain. I'll get down there on my own."

"What? Those friends of yours are going to drive you to the jail? Now you're the one who's kidding."

"I'll *be* there," I shot back at him. "But I'll handle this in my own way." Then I pressed the disconnect button and held it until I knew Ian would be gone. I didn't need his lectures or his sarcasm, not ever, and certainly not now.

I had to walk back to the den to put the phone back in its cradle. I had to tell them I was leaving, somehow.

I guess when I got there the shock was written on my face. "What's the matter, Lib?" Shelley asked me. "You look like you've seen a ghost."

I looked at their faces — Shelley, Debbie, the others — grinning up at me as if this were one more joke, one more goofy thing that Libby had come up with just for laughs.

"No, not that," I said. "It's just that I've got to get home. My father is —" I couldn't say it. I couldn't begin to tell them the truth. I couldn't even bear to look at them anymore, knowing they'd never understand.

"My father is sick," I lied. Then I practically ran out of Shelley's house, wondering if they'd ever have me back in after the news came out.

16

· · · · · · · · ·

Ian

It is the hypocrisy of earthlings that bothers me the most. I can understand their propensity for violence, their sexual drives, their striving for idiotic goals — but I will never understand their hypocrisy. That's what put Rick in jail, nothing else.

Now I suppose even an alien, such as yours truly, could accept hypocrisy as an idiosyncrasy, as a peculiar cultural trait on a planet that does not value women much and limits men a great deal. But it is the righteousness that is so offensive. The moral high horse that various religious leaders climb on, and then leave at the barn when they want to sneak to the milk store for a *Penthouse* — that is what I cannot accept.

Nor can I accept what earthling society did to my father. My father is not a purveyor of pornography just because he sold an underground magazine that was enthusiastic about gay sex. My father's crime is to be different, to refuse to adopt the attitudes that "respectable" society demands. He thumbs his nose at them, quietly meditating, selling books, eating vegetables. So naturally he gets in trouble with the law.

I was at Granny's when Rick called from the holding center. I needed some cash for this plan I had for Missing Link, but I was carefully explaining that I needed new clothes — a more acceptable expenditure — when Granny noticed that one of the cats had knocked the phone over. She put the handset back on, and the phone rang almost immediately.

"Yes," she said. I wasn't paying too much attention, busy with this elaborate story I had concocted so I could buy a tape recorder. Besides, there were three cats tearing at various parts of my body, perhaps made curious by alien flesh. "Again?" she went on. "For what? No! Pshaw." Granny is one of the few people still alive who can say "pshaw" effectively.

"Ian," Granny said, hanging up the phone, "your father has been arrested. For pornography."

"For what?"

"Selling pornography. I don't have the details. Could you run down to the jail and tell him I'm on my way? I'll have to get in touch with my lawyer and post a bond."

"For porn?"

"That's what he said. Now scoot, and be quick about it. Here's money for a taxi and just tell him that I'm coming." She had a look of annoyance on her face. I think the look on mine was more like astonishment. I recovered enough to call Libby, then called a taxi to take me the five miles to where Rick was being held.

Our local jail is relatively new, which is to say less than a hundred years old. It doesn't have obvious jail markings like bars on the windows. Instead it has an architecture much like my high school: gray, cold, fortresslike. I walked inside and the air was heavy with disinfectant. Obviously the jailers were making a failing effort at keeping things clean. The big problem was in most of the people they had to arrest.

I gave my name to some cop sitting up behind a glass partition. He gave me a look as if every second sentence he heard was a lie. I responded with my best earthling smile.

About fifteen minutes later, I was sent through a visual search, a metal detector, and an X-ray machine. These discovered change from the taxi, a Swiss army knife, and every filling I ever had. Then I was led into a small room where Rick was already waiting. He looked remarkably peaceful.

I wasn't sure how I looked, but his first words clued me in.

"Ian, don't be so upset."

"I'm not upset," I told him. Aliens do not get upset. Look at Mr. Spock. Does he ever do more than raise a single eyebrow? "But the smell of this place is pretty awful — like stepping inside a Lysol bottle. How can you stand it?"

"I've been meditating," he said.

"Really?"

"Yeah. They put me in a cell with a couple burglars, some kid who was liberating tires, and a guy who won't tell anybody what he did. It seemed like a better place to meditate than to talk."

"I guess."

"Besides, they all think my crime was pretty despicable."

"What is your crime?" I asked him. "What is this stupid charge, anyhow?"

"There is no real crime, Ian. It's all a political

scheme to shut me down. So long as I was a crazy left-wing propaganda pusher, nobody cared. But when I went mainstream, I became dangerous, so they —" Rick was cut off when there was a knock at the door. Apparently we didn't have to say anything because the door immediately opened with a clunk.

One of the guards showed Granny in.

"My goodness, Ricky — the smell is just dreadful!" Granny said.

"It's decaying human beings," Rick said.

"And the bail. Five thousand dollars. I couldn't believe it. You'd think you were charged with premeditated murder."

"It's politically inspired," Rick said, repeating his earlier line for Granny's benefit.

"Pshaw. And when I think that the district attorney is on the board of the Humane Society, well . . ."

" 'Under a government that imprisons any man unjustly, the true place for a just man is also a prison,' " Rick intoned.

"And who said that?" Granny asked him.

"Thoreau."

"Wasn't he the one who spent a year in some shack sitting by a lake?" Granny asked. I think it was a rhetorical question, because she left no time for an answer. "Sometimes I wish you'd choose your quotations from someone who wasn't a social outcast."

"Thoreau was arrested for not paying taxes," I broke in. "He disagreed with slavery, so —"

Granny shut down my history lesson. "Taxes are not the same as obscenity. That's the charge, Ricky — purveying obscenity. What on earth are you doing in that bookstore?"

Both of us looked at my father.

116

"It must have been the underground newspapers, but I'm still not sure. The censorship laws are so vague, it could be almost anything. The cops don't even have to explain what they found until the court case. You see, the real issue here is freedom of expression."

"Always a cause, Ricky. Always a cause." Granny sighed.

There was another knock on the door, this time from the jail side. A guard stuck his nose in and announced that the bail bond had been arranged. Rick had to be deprocessed and he could leave. My father went out with the guard, giving us a peace sign as he went. Granny and I went back to the waiting room, shaking our heads.

"Five thousand dollars for selling a few magazines," Granny said.

"Now that's obscenity," I told her.

Only earthlings could come up with something so absurd. That's all I could think about on the way home. No wonder Thoreau went off to live by himself. Why would any sensible being want to spend more time with the hypocritical earthlings in Concord? In our society, we are free to look at anything we want, but we have to watch our words, and above all the color of our thoughts. My father simply refused to do that self-censorship. His whole life was a kind of earthling obscenity. Perhaps mine, too.

The awful irony, though, is that my father was not the one to suffer most from the bust, the brief jailing, and the court case. Nor did it really mean that much to Granny and me.

It was Libby who got hurt the most.

17

· · · · · · · · ·

Libby

I knew it would be a disaster as soon as Ian told me where Rick was. It didn't matter if it wasn't fair or if Granny bailed him out or even if he was acquitted in court. None of that would change what was going to happen to me.

Rick gave me the details when he and Ian got back from the jail.

"Obscenity?" was all I could say. I was in a daze. "Didn't you know some of that stuff would get you in trouble?" I asked Rick.

"I was warned," he said flatly.

"So you just waited until they decided to charge you. You couldn't even warn the rest of us." Oh, I was getting mad, mad at the whole world.

"It's freedom of expression, Libby," Ian broke in. He had tracked snow into the house, leaving brown puddles from the door to the kitchen.

"It's just plain stupid!" I shouted. "Why do you have to volunteer to be the local test case on censorship?"

"I didn't ask the police to bust me, Libby," Rick said while I fumed. "I just wouldn't back down when they asked me to take a whole pile of books and magazines off the shelves."

"So why not?" I asked him. "Haven't you ever heard of compromise?"

Ian stared at me with disgust. Maybe that's when I realized I was starting to sound like my mother.

"Some things," Rick said slowly, "are too basic to compromise. Sometimes you have to take a stand."

That stopped me. I looked at him as he stood there, determined, and knew that I respected that part of my father. Maybe I even loved that part of him. He didn't compromise and he didn't back down when it counted.

If only the rest of us didn't have to take a stand beside him.

When the newspaper came out the next day, my father's arrest had made the front page. There was a picture of Rick being led into the police station and another shot of the underground newspapers in the store. The headline read PORN CHARGES LAID and there was even an editorial: "City Gets Tough on Porn — It's About Time." Obviously this was somebody's crusade. My father was being made out to be a dark and dangerous heathen, and the good citizens of our city were going to slaughter him.

The phone rang as soon as I put the paper down. I hoped it would be Shelley, calling to say how awful it must be for me, but it turned out to be Rabbit. I hadn't spoken to her in more than a week, and now this.

"Libby, you must be ready to *die*," she said.

"Why?" I replied, as if I didn't know.

"Your father," she said.

"It's just a trumped-up charge to get somebody elected or something," I said.

"But . . . pornography?" The word finally came out, as if it were dripping with slime.

"It's no big deal," I said, trying to sound like I didn't care. "The charges will never stand up in court."

"No big deal!" Rabbit cried. "Even my parents are talking about it. And you should have seen the evening news. They got your father going into jail and, I mean, he didn't even cover up his face."

"Why should he?"

"Well, don't you think he'd be a little ashamed?"

"Ashamed!" Now I was mad. How could anybody talk to me like this?

"Well, no offense. It doesn't mean anything about you. He's just your father," Rabbit said, suddenly defensive.

"He's got no reason to be ashamed," I shot back. "You can pick up worse trash at the local milk store. Real sexist garbage that degrades women in every fold-out picture. At least the stuff in my dad's bookstore had to be *read*."

"Oh," Rabbit said. "I didn't think about it like that."

"Well, think about it," I told her, and slammed the phone down.

Then *I* thought about it. I couldn't believe Rick's stupidity. The new store had just gotten off the ground, just begun to make money — and then this.

The phone rang again and I picked it up.

"Hello," I said, none too friendly.

"Got any kinky books, eh?" There was some gig-

120

gling. "Go *** yourself . . ." The voice was going on, so I hung up.

The phone rang again but I unplugged it. I took one more look at the newspaper on the couch, then plugged in the phone and dialed Shelley's number. I knew what would happen. I knew it before I called, but still I had to try.

"Shelley?"

"Oh, hi." Her voice sounded a long way away.

"It's me."

"Yeah. You know, Lib, you just caught me in the middle of something."

"Well, call me back," I said.

"I'm going to be tied up tonight," Shelley said.

"I just wanted to talk about what happened."

"I can imagine," she said. "But I'm in a bit of a hurry right now."

"Okay. Well, I guess I'll see you in school tomorrow."

"I guess," she said and hung up the phone.

Shelley didn't even say good-bye.

I sat there for a couple of minutes with the phone in my hand. My life was falling apart around me. All that work, all that effort to get in the group, and now . . .

I dialed again.

"Debbie?"

"No," the voice said back. I recognized it as her mother. "Who is this?"

"It's Libby."

"Libby McNaughton?"

She knew my last name well enough. "Yes. Can I speak to Debbie, please?"

"I'm afraid not, Libby. She's busy studying and won't be answering the phone."

Debbie studying? Who did she think she was fooling? Maybe I should take her on. Maybe I should tell her that I wasn't the same as my father, that I wouldn't stand being treated like this.

But I didn't.

"Oh. Well, tell her I called."

"Of course," she said, sickly sweet. I could almost see the phony smile over the phone.

We both hung up.

So that's how it was going to be. Suddenly everybody would be too busy, just so caught up with one thing or another. And I would be a nonperson.

"What's the matter, Libby?"

I shook off my thoughts and saw Ian at the other side of the room. He was looking down at me, or that's how it seemed.

"Nothing," I said, turning away.

The phone rang. I did nothing. I just sat there as it rang and rang.

Ian came over to answer it. He picked up the receiver and listened silently. I knew what kind of call it was.

Then Ian grinned. "Well, sir," he said into the phone, "I'm certainly pleased that you know how to breathe. Maybe when you learn how to talk we can have a real chat."

I couldn't even smile. Maybe that little routine was supposed to cheer me up, but it didn't work.

Ian shook his head and walked to the kitchen. I just sat there. I didn't have enough energy to move.

Then the phone rang again. I stared at it like it was

some kind of monster. I felt like all my problems were wrapped up in this one plastic box. I hated it. I hated everything.

I grabbed the receiver and shouted, "Why don't you just stop it! Stop it and leave us alone, you —"

But my words were stopped by a quiet voice on the other end. It was my mom.

"Libby? What's wrong?"

For a few seconds I couldn't speak. The long-distance line crackled. I tried to make my voice work again. Say something, say anything.

"Are you all right?" my mother asked after a while.

"No," I said. "I'm not all right. I'm . . . nothing. I'm nothing!"

And then I started crying. Long-distance tears, all the way to California.

18

· · · · · · · · ·

Ian

Libby and I both had to deal with some of the less pleasant earthling reactions — scorn, derision, ridicule, ostracism. She pretended, of course, that none of this bothered her. But I know it bothered *me,* and I'm not even an aspiring human. Besides, I was just in the kitchen when she broke down on the phone to Sharon, and that was before the worst had begun.

Apparently Libby was being treated like an inmate from a leper colony out on a day pass. People just stayed away — far away — from the possible source of infection. I saw Libby in the cafeteria, eating her lunch alone, not even Rabbit venturing to sit beside her. I felt so sorry for Libby that I almost went over and offered to eat lunch with her. But I figured that a gesture like that would be somewhat worse on her Richter scale of personal disaster than eating lunch by herself.

I was treated pretty much like Libby, but I had been immunized to that through elementary school. I already knew I was a moral disease, a creature from under a rock, a threat to truth, justice, and the American Way. For someone who's already an alien, it's hard to feel more alienated — all puns intended. Unlike Libby, I did not have a whole circle of friends to lose. I only had one friend, R.T., and he stuck with me. In fact, I managed to convince him of the hypocrisy of society and the absurdity of the charge in a ten-minute discussion. It was just a matter of being objective.

Unfortunately, simpler minds, like Missing Link's, tend to be very subjective. To Missing Link, I was no longer just a moonkid. Since Rick's arrest, I had become a "fag" and a "pervert," to use two of the more printable expressions. He had a great deal of support in these assertions from the other Cro-Magnon types and most of the girls, even my favorite, Marci, the one with large breasts.

Following a great earthling tradition of persecution, Missing Link decided to eliminate me from the face of the earth.

"He's gonna kill you" is how R.T. phrased it.

"Why?"

"Because of your dad. He says you're scum and he's going to wipe you out."

"Why?" I repeated.

"Because," R.T. said. It's a word that earthlings use to mean, It's self-evident.

"Oh," I replied, which I use to mean, Seems crazy to me but that's the way it is.

Of course, Missing Link was simply threatening to do precisely what most people in our community wanted to do. Never forget — earthlings will tolerate people who are different if and only if (a) they keep their differences private, (b) they feel guilty, and (c) they have money. Preferably, as they say in math, all three conditions should be met.

We McNaughtons — or at least two of us — were public, unashamed, and poor. Hence I was going to be dead.

I preferred otherwise. Fortunately, most of my Operation Cro-Magnon had already been planned out by the time of the bust. I had begun spending time at the university in November, partly because it was on one of the diversionary routes home that let me avoid confrontations with Missing Link, partly because I liked it there. I prefer humans with books and running shoes to those with T-shirts and tattoos.

I found out that there were groups at the university who played adventure games on campus — or under the campus, depending on how serious they got. Our local paper, before it began running editorials about Rick's Bookroom, had run a few stories on this peculiarity of university life, Dungeons & Dragons in real life. I think the intention was to show the unwashed masses that the university could be as dangerous a place as the sidewalk outside Clancy's tavern, a fact that should be evident to almost anyone by now. At the time, I stuck the article in the back of my mind, wondering if it would ever be useful. By December, I decided that "ever" was right now.

I went underground. The newspaper had said there was an entrance to the tunnels from someplace in the engineering building. That was easy enough to find. A plastic card to jimmy the lock and I was into a long passageway. This first tunnel was a large one and relatively clean. I could stand up all the way through and didn't have to get too close to the steam pipes, which were why the tunnels existed. The passage was hot and damp, but not otherwise unpleasant for a relatively small alien like me. I became convinced, down there, that my home planet must have a climate like Venus.

The first tunnel ended under the philosophy building with a little room off to one side where the students had set up a card table. I could picture the undergraduates sneaking down to play D & D or some real-life version of the game. The walls certainly had more literate graffiti than what one might expect from custodians and pipe fitters.

To the left of the little room with the table was another tunnel, but this one was much smaller than the first. And there was no light. I couldn't explore it until the weekend, equipped with my scuzziest jeans and a flashlight. But this tunnel was precisely what I had in mind for Missing Link — small, cramped, hot. If I were claustrophobic, I would have gone crazy in there. I had to move along on my hands and knees, trying not to get too close to the pipes just in case the insulation had fallen away and exposed bare, heated metal. The flashlight let me see ahead, but only a short way. The tunnel curved slightly, so after ten minutes of crawling I couldn't see how I'd come in or where the tunnel might end.

Not a nice feeling.

I sat there for a second, wondering what I'd do if the flashlight went out or if the tunnel got smaller. It was hot, really hot. Sweat rolled down my face, carrying dirt and grease with it. I heard a sharp hiss from up ahead and pointed my flashlight at where some steam came shooting out of a pipe. Then it was quiet as a tomb.

I kept going. The tunnel took me about twenty minutes to crawl through; then it came up in a manhole not far from Philosopher's Walk. I pushed up the manhole cover and climbed into the frigid air of the upper world.

In the week that followed, I explored a few more of the tunnels and made a map of where they went and where they came out. If I couldn't lure Missing Link to the right place, I wanted to have some options. The other tunnels led almost to the dormitories, under the administration building, over to the reactor, and stopped just short of the gym. I suppose there were others that I didn't find. Everywhere I went, I saw the marks that students before me had left. The rumor in the paper was that some kids had gone down and never come up, trapped inside by steam, darkness, and tight space. Though I never came across a body, the rumor struck me as more reasonable than most.

After our Christmas visit to California, I had perfected my plan. When Missing Link vowed to destroy me as soon as his leg permitted him the mobility, I wasn't worried. I knew I'd be ready. And R.T. would be with me.

The month or so leading up to Easter was probably the worst. Our local paper had decided to make pornography some kind of issue, and seized on Rick as the scapegoat. This continuing attention and the various court maneuvers kept things at a rolling boil. Rick kept running his store, drawing more customers than ever, though some must have been disappointed to find André Gide instead of hard-core pornography, and I kept going to school. Rick suffered from obscene phone calls, death threats, and the occasional picket. I suffered ostracism, jeers, and Missing Link.

Naturally, Rick and I drew together.

"Are you getting tired of it all?" I asked Rick one evening. He had been meditating more than usual since the bust, but looked as ragged after the meditations as he did before them.

"I can't clear my head."

"Neither can I," I said, flopping down in the bean-bag chair. There is a kind of continuing tension in knowing that somebody wants to kill you. It's enough to get even an alien down.

"I'm worried about Libby," Rick said. He sounded worn out and looked exhausted. "She's taken this harder than any of us. It's like she's not really with us anymore."

"Libby's just upset about losing her stuck-up friends," I said. "She hooked up with a bunch of snobs and now they dropped her. It was inevitable."

"But the bust is what brought it on."

"They would have dropped her sooner or later anyhow," I told him. "Libby's not really like them. She's too much a McNaughton."

"I don't know if that's true anymore." Rick looked away, his eyes focused way off in the distance. "She's been talking to Sharon on the phone every other day."

I nodded. We both knew what that was about.

"You know, Ian, if Libby wants to leave, I can't stop her." Rick's gaze dropped back to the floor.

"She wouldn't back out on us. Not now," I said in my most reassuring voice. "We're all taking a stand together, just like always."

I was trying to sound hopeful and reasonable and strong. But maybe I was just covering up some deeper fears. I didn't know, for instance, if in standing together I should have said "all" or just "both of us."

19

. . . .

Libby

April was the cruelest month of my entire life. Everything had fallen apart, but I was still going around with my head up, trying to pretend it was all okay. I still wore my California clothes to school. I pretended that I had dropped Eddie for a boy in California. I acted as if the group weren't good enough for *me,* and not the other way around.

But inside I was a mess.

I don't know which was worse, the strangers or the former friends. The strangers at school would whisper about me, sometimes pointing. Conversations would suddenly stop when I came close. Little jokes about my father and the bookstore would slip into a class discussion; then the strangers would giggle and then there'd be silence.

The silence was the worst part. That's what I couldn't get used to. Debbie and Shelley, my friends — my former friends — were masters of silence. They didn't treat me like someone they wanted to avoid, but like somebody who didn't exist. They looked *through* me when we passed in the halls. They sat in the cafeteria — Shelley, Debbie, Eddie, Bill, all of them — laughing and looking perfect, just the way they always did. I sat at the other end, usually alone, sometimes lucky enough to have lunch with Rabbit.

You see, I had a *reputation.* Ordinarily, the way you get a *reputation* in high school is by doing something sexual, but I had managed to develop a *reputation* without having done anything more than kiss a boy good night. I had inherited one. Other kids inherit college tuition or a car or a trunk full of clothes; I inherited a *reputation* for being a pornographer's daughter.

"No offense," Rabbit said. "Not that it has anything to do with you as a person." Rabbit was convinced that my father was an unrepentant sinner for selling dirty books, but decided that I could still be saved.

"Of course not," I said.

"It's like Shelley's father — he's rich and so she's rich. Well, they look at your father and he's . . . well, and so they think you're the same way."

"Yeah, well, maybe they should learn that Shelley's father is paying bribe money to half the city council and he's got a connection to the Mafia and —"

"It doesn't matter, Libby," Rabbit broke in. "She's rich and he's respectable. Your family . . ." Rabbit could never bring herself to actually say out loud the nasty thoughts she kept in her head. "I mean, if that Bob Guccione guy was your father, it might be okay."

"Yeah, million-dollar porn is okay but selling one three-buck gay magazine puts you in jail."

"Look, Libby, you can't expect kids to be rational. They've all gone crazy."

132

I tried to keep myself above all this, pretending so hard that I didn't notice. But oh, it hurt. There were days when I came home from school and cried, others when I just stared out the window for hours. I stopped answering the phone. I stopped hoping that it would all blow over. I tried to stop thinking altogether.

I guess Ian and Rick were having their own problems. I don't know. I was so busy dealing with my own, pretending I was okay, that I didn't pay too much attention to theirs.

"You're not the only one having a hard time," Ian told me one night.

"What makes you think I'm having a hard time?" I shot back.

"I saw you at lunch today, alone."

"Maybe I like to eat alone."

"Libby, why are you trying to cover it up? You've been dropped. You're a social hot potato — just like Rick and me."

"I am not," I spat at him. "I may be having a hard time, but I'm not like you two. I'm not a weirdo or an alien. I'm . . . I'm normal and I'm going to beat this thing."

Obviously I couldn't talk to Ian. He and my father seemed to enjoy being outcasts. They didn't understand. Only my mother understood.

I told her everything. Two or three times a week, on the phone, spilling my guts. I told her what the kids were saying about me, about Rick. I told her how I'd been dropped by the group and everybody else. I told her how lonely I was, how miserable.

And she understood. She knew I was hanging on by my fingernails. She had been through the same thing — the drug bust, the moves from house to house, the separation and divorce. She told me that I was strong enough to survive. That I should keep my chin up, whatever happened.

Then in May, my mom flew in on her way to New York. It was two weeks before the court case and I was still a mess inside. My mom said she wanted to see me, and Ian, too, if he could come, but especially me. She was worried about us.

I really wanted to see her, but not with Ian along. I think I mentioned it to him like this — "You don't really want to go out to the airport just to see Sharon for two hours, do you?" And I was relieved when he said no, mumbling something about being busy at the university. Besides, he said that Mom didn't really want to see him. I objected to that at the time, but I also knew that he was right. Mom was coming to see me — to talk to *me.*

I took the day off from school, something I'd been doing more often than not lately. I slept till ten, washed my hair, tried to put some color on my face, then grabbed the eleven-thirty bus to the airport. I got out there too early, so I read the paper and some travel brochures about places I would never visit. I felt good just hanging around there, the sun streaming in through big plate-glass windows, me pretending I was about to hop a plane to the Virgin Islands. School was so depressing these days, but the airport seemed full of dreams.

My mom's plane came in at one twenty-five, right on time, and she came up the ramp about ten minutes later, looking wonderful. Her hair was lighter than when I had seen her at Christmas, her skin glowed, and her clothes had a kind of flash that we don't see around here. I threw my arms around her when she got to me, holding her tighter than ever.

"Libby, you're crying," she said when I let go.

"Really?" I said. I didn't feel the tears, but my cheeks were wet. "I guess I must be glad to see you."

"Well, I'm glad to be with you. You've been through such a rough time."

"It's been horrible," I corrected. "It's still horrible."

"Come on, let's go get some lunch and we can talk."

We walked over to the nicer restaurant at the airport, the one with the salad bar on one side and tables overlooking the runways on the other. My mom just had a drink because she'd eaten on the plane. I tried to stuff myself since my weight had begun to slip down again.

We spent a lot of time going through what had already happened. I told her some things about the court case that we had heard from our Civil Liberties Union lawyer. He figured that the local judge might uphold the charges, but that we'd certainly win on the appeal.

"Libby, it doesn't matter if Rick wins the case," my mom said.

"But it's got to," I said. After all the grief we'd been through, it had to be important.

"No, it doesn't matter because the other side has already won. Even if they drop the charges. The damage has already been done to you and Ian."

"Damage?"

"To your reputation, your growth. This is a pretty crucial time in your life. You should be — I don't know how to say this — blossoming, turning into a woman. You shouldn't have to be some kind of social misfit with no friends and no social life. It isn't fair."

"I know it isn't."

"That's why I think you should come out with us."

"For a vacation?"

"For good."

She was looking right at me, saying just what I thought she was going to say, and suddenly I got scared. I got confused. I looked off, over the runways.

"Rick might be let off," I said quietly.

"It doesn't matter," she replied. "Whether Rick wins or loses, I think you should come live with us. Finish high school in California. You deserve it, Libby. You deserve better than what you've got here. You've got a right to have boyfriends and a social life and a good time. You shouldn't have to worry about a father who just goes from one cause to another. Come out with us and you'll get a chance to be the *you* that you've always wanted."

"But school . . ." I said. I wasn't sure why. It wasn't that I even cared that much about school, but something inside was tugging at me.

"Come at the end of June. You'll have something to look forward to, and that'll make the next month go faster." She was smiling as if everything were so simple.

"Ian will never come," I said.

"Maybe not now, but he can come later if he wants. You can't spend your life just worrying about Ian and Rick. It's time you thought about yourself. What do *you* want? Do you want to stay here and be an outcast because of your father? Do you want to keep on sacrificing yourself because your brother and your father won't grow up?"

"I don't know." Something inside was telling me it wasn't that simple.

"Libby, I know you can't give me an answer right now. I just want you to think about it. Things could get really bad in a few weeks when the case hits the courts, and I wanted you and Ian to know that you have options. The bedroom is there and ready for you. There's an extra car if you want one. There's a high school down at the bottom of the hill. We have everything you could possibly want."

"It sounds too good to be true," I said.

"It can be that good," she said, reaching out to squeeze my hand. Her fingers were cold from the ice in her drink. "We want you with us."

20

· · · · · · · · ·

Ian

I couldn't go to the airport because that was the day
R.T. and I had set for Operation Cro-Magnon. We
probably had postponed it too long already. Just the
week before, Missing Link and two of his fellow barbarians attempted to ambush R.T. and me on the way
home from school. I managed to outrun them, but
R.T. wasn't so lucky.

Now it is one thing for Missing Link and his bron-
tosauran friends to go after me. That was understand-
able, given the pattern of evolution that had left them
with monstrous bodies and minuscule brains. Naturally they regarded me as a danger to their species.
Naturally they wanted to destroy me. But why pick
on R.T.? The poor kid's only problem was that he
had stuck with me as a friend. Surely even the most
primitive mind couldn't use that as an excuse to alter
R.T.'s face the way they did.

By Tuesday, R.T. had healed up and was ready. I had
the equipment in place and was ready myself. All sys-
tems were go, as earthlings say before a space launch.

What I had to do to set my plan in motion was annoy both Mrs. Proctor and Missing Link, an easy enough feat even for an earthling. I managed to get Missing Link fired up with a clever insult or two, then got Mrs. Proctor to give me a detention because I wouldn't apologize. Missing Link finished the day ready to kill me; Mrs. Proctor unwittingly played right into my plan.

At four o'clock, Mrs. Proctor sent me off with the usual threats and attempts to produce guilt. I smiled, oozed contrition, and got ready for what counted.

Operation Cro-Magnon was beginning. *Stage One.* Reel them in. I was the lure; they were the fish. Thank goodness fish are so stupid.

Missing Link, Marco, and a behemoth named Randy were waiting for me on the other side of the back doors. The inset of the doors made them a little less visible, but the cigarette smoke was a dead giveaway. It was hard for me to keep up my "unsuspecting" look and not burst out laughing.

I walked a few steps until I was sure they had seen me, then ducked the other way, toward the elementary school. Now Missing Link would either have to run after me or sneak around to the playground for an ambush. A quick look behind showed that I wasn't being followed. I could relax until I reached the playground, where Missing Link and his friends would "surprise" me.

Or I would surprise them.

I strolled through the playground, innocent as could be. I returned a ball to some little kids who were playing a game. Then I skipped over the hopscotch markings on the asphalt. Cool and dumb, I was.

And then I was "surprised." The three of them stepped out in front of me from the only spot where they could have been hiding. They were smiling.

"Okay, fag," came the wonderfully ignorant voice.

"A fag in England refers to the end of a cigarette," I said. "I don't happen to have one. But I do have this." I reached into my pack and pulled out a squirt gun.

The three of them started laughing.

"Oh, kill me," called out Randy.

That wasn't what I had in mind. I squeezed the squirt gun trigger and shot a stream onto Randy.

"Hey, this stings," he said as it hit his face.

"Dilute acetic acid," I explained, turning the gun on the others. I sprayed just enough vinegar on the three of them to blind them for a minute. Then I took off while they were busy trying to rub the stuff out of their eyes.

The first stage was successful. I had a one-block lead and they were mad enough to follow me anywhere for revenge. *Stage Two* was beginning. Get them to the university.

I ran. They ran after me.

Four blocks to go.

Three blocks.

Two blocks. The three of them are getting closer. Marco can run fast, faster than me. Faster than I expect. I look back and see the expression on his face. He wants to kill me. Me.

I'm running out of breath. I've practiced this run for a month, but now I can't seem to go fast enough. My feet are still moving, but so slowly, as if I'm barely going faster than a walk. I force my arms to pump, my legs to move.

Until I trip on a curb. The fall sends me flying onto a lawn, scraping my shoulder against a tree.

I scramble to get up on my feet, but Marco is on top of me. His heavy breathing is so close I can feel it. I bring my knee up into his stomach and he rolls off. Now I've got enough time to crawl away.

But they're right behind me. My breath is burning in my lungs. I hadn't planned on this, having them so close. How many blocks to go? I've lost count. People are watching us as we run, thinking this is a game. They don't know these guys want to kill me.

We reach the university gates and tear past the guardhouse. I run up the gentle rise, duck through some pine trees, then run across the lawn leading to Stage Three. If only I can make it. Missing Link and the others are close, so close I can't even slow down to look behind me. My feet are slipping on the wet grass, but they haven't caught me yet.

Up ahead is the engineering building. If I can make it inside, to the tunnel, I'll be all right. I run up to the front doors, see the three of them reflected in the glass, hear them shouting. Inside, it's dark. Hard to see until my eyes adjust, but I know where I'm going. Now I've got the advantage.

And I'm going to use it.

I zip to the right and wait for a second at the stairwell. When Missing Link and the others pour through the door, I jump down the stairs two at a time. Now I'm in the basement corridor. Where's the door? Just where it always is. Why am I so scared?

I race to the tunnel door. A quick squeeze and it pulls open. I zip inside. The lights are already glowing down the first part of the tunnel.

Stage Three. I'm halfway down the tunnel when the

Cro-Magnons come inside. I'm having a hard time catching my breath, but that doesn't matter. Now the operation really begins.

"We've got him," Missing Link tells the others. His voice is out of breath but full of assurance.

"You're dead, Moonkid," Marco says to me.

"A rat. He's a rat caught in a tunnel." Randy laughs.

The three of them start coming toward me, Missing Link in the lead. The tunnel is so narrow that they have to come single file.

I back away from them, just as I've practiced. My breathing is slowing down now, my mind working again. I have to lure them ahead, just beyond the curve. There, I've got them that far.

I climb over a ledge of bricks to lead them into the smaller tunnel, the one with only a few lights. Slowly they come after me, but their size is against them, and the darkness. I know the tunnel by feel. Not too far ahead, just off to the right, is the ladder. I feel for the break in the wall, feel my way into the pitch-black side chamber, feel the ladder in my hand.

The others are way behind me now, slowed up by the cramped space, the darkness. I climb up the ladder and am ready to surface when I hear them shout.

"Hey, who turned off the lights?"

R.T. has done his first job. Now if he does the second, they're trapped. I wait for the sound — the metal door rolling across the passage. Rumble. Slam.

I open the manhole over my head, pop through the opening, then slam the lid down. I race along the surface, knowing the three of them are trapped in the darkness beneath my feet.

I go into the engineering building through its rear door, then run down the stairs to meet R.T. He's just outside the door to the tunnel.

"Everything okay?" I ask him.

"You were late. I thought they got you."

"Almost did. Good thing you were all set here."

Stage Four. R.T. and I go back into the tunnel, flashlights ready.

We can hear the three bozos in the tunnel. One of them is crying. Missing Link tells him to shut up. Then somebody starts swearing. I think he was burned on one of the steam pipes.

I pick up the cardboard megaphone I had hidden the night before. "Hey, you," I shout into the tunnel. My voice bounces along the walls, reverberating through the tunnel.

The kid who's crying suddenly stops. It's dead quiet. Nothing but the hiss of the steam pipes.

"You're trapped," I say to them. R.T. starts to giggle but I punch him in the arm to keep him quiet.

"Turn on the lights, Ian. Enough's enough," says Missing Link.

"You three are going to die," I tell them.

"Let me out of here," begs one kid. It's the one who's crying. "I can't stand this. I can't," he says, blubbering.

I give R.T. the signal to start recording all this on his Walkman. Then I speak through the megaphone. "You're trapped, Donald Fraser. So are you, Marco, and you, Randy. Now I want the truth or I'll turn on the steam."

The tunnel is hot already, hot enough to make sweat pour down my face even in the larger section. I can picture the three of them slowly roasting inside the smaller tunnel.

"Stop kidding around," says Missing Link.

"Just let us out," says the crying one.

"Come on, Ian," says the last voice, Randy's. So Marco had cracked first.

I hear a hiss of escaping steam and Missing Link swears, scalded by one of the pressure valves.

I begin again. "There'll be more of that unless you do what I say. Now I want an apology from all three of you. And I want a promise that you won't come after me or my friends ever again. And I want it now." My order echoes through the tunnel.

"I'm sorry, Ian," cries Marco, his voice shaking. "I didn't want to do anything. It was Don. I won't do it again. Honest."

I hear a slap and a cry. Then Don shouts out and there's another sound, a groan.

"What about you, Randy?" I say.

"Just let us out."

"Apologize!" Thunder through the megaphone.

"For what? We didn't do nothing."

Stage Five: terror. "All right," I shout, "turn on the steam."

R.T. is up ahead at the first escape valve. He gives the handle a few turns and steam begins hissing into the tunnel.

Farther in, Marco is going crazy. He's crying and screaming. Missing Link tells him to shut up, but I can hear that the big guy is cracking, too.

"You've got five minutes before the gas reaches you," I say.

"All right," Randy cries. "I'm sorry. We won't touch you, not ever again. Now turn it off."

"No," I shout. "I want Fraser to talk. Give up and I'll set you free."

"Dream on, Moonkid," Missing Link shouts back.

He's tougher than I thought. R.T. comes back and asks if we should stop. I shake my head. I want more of this. I can't help it — I want to destroy them.

"You want more?" I boom at them. "Then here it comes."

I nod to R.T., who plugs in an electric drill. The whine is deafening in the tunnel, like a chain saw. I start moving down the tunnel so that the sound will seem to be coming at them. That does it.

"All right," Missing Link shouts. It's hard to make out the words over the drill, the steam, and Marco's crying. "I'm sorry."

I turn off the drill.

"Say it again."

"I said I'm sorry. Just let us out and we won't bug you again."

"Beg me," I boom at him. I'm getting carried away. Something inside me is running this operation, something that scares even me. "Beg me or else." I signal R.T. and he turns on the drill again.

From the tunnel I can hear fighting. It seems like Randy and Marco are ganging up on Missing Link. Then a voice cries out.

"I'm begging you," the voice says. It's Missing Link's.

R.T. turns off the drill. He wants to go, but I'm not done yet.

"One more thing," I say. "Which of you trashed my father's bookstore?"

"We don't know nothing," Missing Link says.

"Talk or you'll die down here. Who did it?"

145

There's a scuffle, then Marco's voice sings out, "It was Randy and Don and Don's brother. That's the truth. Now let us out of here."

"Do you admit it, Donald Fraser?" I ask. I check to make sure R.T.'s Walkman is recording all this.

There's a grunt. Somebody punched somebody.

"Yeah," Missing Link shouts. "I did it. We all did it. Now let us go."

I nod and R.T. turns off the Walkman. Operation completed.

"Bye-bye," I say, laughing at them, then flip on the lights.

R.T. and I race up the stairs and over to the philosophy building. There is a classroom that looks right over the lawn to engineering. It will give us a good view of the three Cro-Magnons when they come out.

And stumble out they finally do. I watch them walk off and suddenly feel cold. The smile disappears from my face. This is my moment of victory, isn't it? I should feel righteous and triumphant. But the feeling in my chest isn't like that; it's gray and ugly. And the taste in my mouth is worse.

21

. . . .

Libby

Ian came in late that day, covered with dirt. The filth didn't surprise me. I knew he was involved in something down in the tunnels of the university, probably something weird, and I really didn't care what it was. Compared to me, with my problems, Ian was still just a carefree little kid.

But that day there was something different about Ian. Even my father noticed it. He looked up from the steaming wok on the stove when Ian came in and saw that something was wrong.

"Ian, uh . . ."

Then Rick stopped. There was this look on Ian's face like he was going to cry. That was the strangest thing. I couldn't remember the last time Ian cried. When the kids used to beat him up, even when Mom left, Ian never cried. Yet Rick stopped talking because Ian might break out in tears. Something had happened to Ian that he couldn't quite handle.

Of course, something was happening to me that I couldn't quite handle. But I had an out. I could get out of all this — walk through the door, take a taxi to the airport, fly to California, and never come back. They had everything for me out there. Why couldn't I just trust that?

Rick went back to stir-frying some vegetables for dinner while Ian went off to clean up. I was left staring at my father, almost examining him. What I saw when I looked at Rick was hair — everywhere. The hair on top of his head was longer than mine and curled just above his shoulders. His beard was thick, like Rasputin's, and grew down below his neck. Even his eyebrows were hairy, some of the hairs so long he had to comb them back out of his eyes.

This was a father? That's what I kept saying to myself when I looked at him. This man with the wild hair and the sad eyes really produced me?

"How's your mother?" Rick asked while I fried up some meat to add to his vegetables.

"She looks good," I said. "She's probably having a nice expense-account dinner in New York tonight. That's the kind of job I'd like to have someday."

"You want the expense account?"

"No, not that. The travel and the meetings and everything."

"No bookstores?" he asked. He was pulling my leg, just like he'd done ever since I was a kid.

"Only if there was a chain of them," I shot back.

Rick just smiled. "See if Ian will come down and eat."

I went out in the hall and hollered up the stairs. Ian grunted something and I heard the floor creak, so I figured he was getting out of bed. By the time food was on the table, Ian had made it down to the kitchen.

"Business was good today," Rick said. I think he was talking to Ian more than to me, but Ian said nothing. "Sold the last backgammon book to some woman who wanted to teach her daughter."

"What was the take?" I asked to break the silence.

"I don't know," Rick said. "Maybe three hundred. I'll add it up when I go back to close up."

"That's way up," I said.

"It's the publicity from the court case," Rick went on. "One guy asked me today if it was all a publicity stunt."

"What did you say?"

"I said it ripped up my kids too much to be worth it."

There was nothing I could reply to that, so the three of us fell into silence. Maybe we should never have tried to force conversation anyhow. Ian was obviously so miserable that nothing was going to make him feel better.

"I don't want to eat any more of this," Ian announced when he had half finished the pile on his plate.

"Something happen today?" Rick asked him. He was trying to make it an idle question, but didn't quite pull it off.

"No, nothing."

"You should have come to see Mom," I said.

"Maybe. Maybe I should have." And off he went, walking up the stairs, his feet heavy on the wooden steps.

Rick and I said nothing until we heard the creak of the floorboards upstairs.

"Libby, you know what's wrong?"

"With Ian?"

He just looked at me as if I were playing dumb for no reason.

"I don't know," I said. "There's some kid at school who wants to beat him up. Why are you so concerned all of a sudden?"

"Maybe I just need a change from worrying about you."

He looked at me in that half-smiling, half-serious way he has. And that ended the conversation. I cleared my plate away. Rick went into the living room for some brief yoga exercises; then he left for the store. The house was quiet. Ian had gone upstairs and hadn't even asked me about Mom. Maybe that's why I went upstairs. Or maybe I was worried about him, too. Or maybe I just wanted to talk, and there was nobody else, anymore, to talk to.

I found Ian lying on his futon, propped up with a pillow. There was a Conan comic book on the floor, but Ian wasn't reading it when I came in. I sat down on the one lousy chair in his room and asked the obvious question. "What's the matter with you, Moonchild?"

Ian didn't answer.

"Earth to Ian. Earth to Ian."

"Cut it out."

"Why? What's with you?"

"Nothing."

"I don't believe it. What happened today? Klingon attack? What?"

"Get real."

"What do you know about real, Moonkid? You're from another planet, right?" I was angry and sarcastic, but he had it coming. He had had it coming for years.

"Leave me alone."

"I've got to tell you what Mom said. She asked me to talk to you."

"I already know," he said. "There are two one-way tickets to California. Right? A bedroom for each of us. Right? Everything will be just great if we cut and run out there. Have I got the whole thing?"

"Yeah," I said, surprised at how much he had figured out.

"I knew the hard sell was coming. Ever since Christmas. But I'm not going and they both know it. What about you? She offer you everything — money, house, private school, a fresh start?"

"And a car," I added.

"Of course, maybe a sports car. It's *you*, Libby."

"Why are you always so cynical, Ian? She's your mother as well as mine. And she's worried about the two of us."

"She wasn't too worried five years ago," Ian shot back. And that connected, because it was true.

"She's worried now. And she wants us to know there are alternatives . . . to this." I looked around the room at his space models and *Enterprise* blueprints and the Albert Einstein poster on the door. The place was a disaster, a mess, just like our lives.

"Message received," Ian said. He rolled over, trying to get me out of there.

"Ian, where *are* you?"

"Nowhere," he said into the wall.

"What happened today?"

Ian was silent for a while, just staring into the wall. He looked strange, tense, and tired all at once. Then he spoke. "I trapped three guys in the tunnels under the university. I wanted to . . . I wanted to scare them right out of their skulls."

"You?"

"R.T. and me. I've been planning it for months. I wanted to get back at them for what they did to me and R.T. and Rick."

"Rick?"

"Yeah. Three of them trashed the bookstore on Halloween. I've got a confession on the tape."

"What tape? How'd you get all this?"

"I tortured them," Ian said quietly.

"How could you?" I said. Ian was only five feet tall and about as fierce as my father.

But Ian took my words the other way. "How could I? That's a good question. That's what's been bothering me ever since. Listen to the tape — listen to what I did."

Ian plugged in his tape recorder and pushed the play button.

Turn on the lights, Ian. Enough's enough.

You three are going to die.

Let me out of here. I can't stand this. I can't . . .

The one kid was sobbing like crazy, really scared out of his head. I felt like I was listening to some sick television show. I wanted to say something, but I kept quiet until Ian turned it off, right after the kids admitted trashing our store.

"That was sick, Ian."

"No, it was human. That's what scares me. You know what I realized when it was all over? What I saw in myself? That I'm just like everybody else. I'm as sick and perverted and sadistic as anybody else on this hideous planet."

"Ian . . ." I said, trying to stop him.

"And you know what it means?" he said, his voice cracking. "It means I'm one of you. Just as stupid and animal as all the rest of you."

"Well, you had reasons."

"That doesn't matter." The words were just pouring out. "I'll tell you what matters. I'll tell you what makes me feel sick about myself. It's not even all the planning and the scheming I did to set the thing up. It was how I felt when I was doing it, when I was torturing them. You know how I felt?"

We just stared at each other.

"I loved it," he whispered. "I had this rush, this rush of power."

"That's sick."

"That's what scares me. It's what's inside me. The human part. I've been hiding from it for too long."

Then he started crying, just like any other kid, any other human kid. The tears came out of the corners of his eyes and rolled down his cheeks. He squinted, trying to hold them back, then lost the fight. The tears came out and his shoulders heaved.

"What am I going to do?" he sobbed.

But I didn't know what to say. Ian wasn't an alien, but he couldn't accept being human. He was nowhere, just like me, and I didn't have an answer for either of us.

22

. . . .

Ian

Humanity! What can I say of this strange species that struts around the earth on two legs, dreaming its wild dreams while trudging through the slog and bog of daily existence? How can I justify its terrible extravagances — its wars, hatred, and violence — except by saying that the species is also capable of charity, heroism, and love? No rational creature circling in space, picking up signals from both "Masterpiece Theater" and "The Dating Game," will be able to understand it; no rational creature living on earth will be able to tolerate all of it, but that contradiction is in the nature of humanity.

And I, too, am part of the species.

That was the admission that was hardest to make. I always knew, at a certain level, that my fantasies of a mother ship and a home planet were about as sensible as Libby's dreams of making it into a magazine feature. But the idea of being an alien, an alien of whatever kind, had an enormous appeal. It meant that when two little kids started fighting in the school play-

154

ground, I could step back and say to myself, *I'm not like that*. It meant that when our President sent troops to such-and-such a place, playing the school bully on a larger playground, I could shake my head and wonder how rational creatures could ever vote for such a man. The tremendous advantage of being an alien is that all the terrible stuff — all that was *not me*. Not my fault. Not my concern. *Beam me up, Scotty, these are all barbarians down here.*

What I discovered that terrible day in the tunnels was a hidden part of myself. All that which I had declared to be *not me* — the violence, the hatred, the fascination with filth and degradation — all that turned out to be part of me as much as it afflicted the rest of humanity. What I did to Missing Link was not, in itself, as horrible as the fact that I enjoyed it. I loved the power, the revenge, the terror, all those emotions we ascribe to Nazis and barbarians, desperately trying to pretend that they are not lurking in all of us.

I dragged myself to school on Thursday, not because I wanted to go, but because I knew it was time to face the real world. I felt small — not just physically small, which has always been the case, but small in some more important way. I walked up to school and saw the usual group of smokers and dopers and hard rocks out in front, but I couldn't look down on them in the old way. The moral elevator shoes I'd been wearing had been replaced with bare feet.

When I reached Mrs. H. Proctor's class, I carefully avoided looking at Missing Link and Marco. They carefully avoided looking at me. I think we were mutually embarrassed by what had happened. They were probably embarrassed about their fear. I was simply embarrassed about what they had seen in me: the delight in their torture, the awful cunning. Someday, maybe, I could tell them that I was sorry, but an admission like that would be a long time in coming. For now, we simply avoided looking at each other.

I had to look at Mrs. H. Proctor. She was irritated that I had missed a day of school and wanted to meet with me at the end of the day.

"Why?" I asked.

"We're meeting in Mr. McDougall's office. I'll explain it to you then."

Information like that was worse than no information. Obviously I had sinned in some serious way to rate a meeting with Mr. McDougall, the vice principal. But how?

"Maybe they found out about Operation Cro-Magnon?" R.T. said at lunch. He sucked in his breath at the very idea of it.

"I don't see how," I said. "Why would Missing Link tell them? Besides, nothing happened on school grounds, so it's really out of their jurisdiction."

"Maybe somebody's parents called up. I mean, when you think about what happened —"

"Do you have to smile when you talk about it?" I asked him.

"Well, it's kind of funny," R.T. said.

"It's *not* funny," I said, trying to emphasize the point. "What we did Tuesday was sick, R.T., and if anybody ever finds out about it, I'll know that you're the one who told."

"I won't say anything," R.T. replied, cowed only for a second by my serious tone. "But, really, they had it coming."

156

"That's what the Crusaders said about the infidels and the Nazis about the Jews."

"Huh?"

"Just remember, nobody ever has it coming like that, okay? Nobody should have the power to drag us down to that level. We've got to set our own level and somehow stay there. You understand?"

"Oh, sure, Ian," he said, nodding so I would believe him. And I tried. I wanted to believe that both R.T. and I had learned something from Operation Cro-Magnon, but I wasn't sure that we had learned the same things.

At the end of the day, I went down to the main office and was sent by the secretary into Mr. Mc-Dougall's cubicle. The vice principal was off somewhere, probably yelling at a kid, and I was to wait. I spent the time looking around at the hopeful little sayings he had posted on the bulletin boards and walls: "Today is the first day of the rest of your life"; "A loser is only a winner who doesn't try"; "Your parents aren't perfect, but neither are you." All of these were embroidered with flowers or cherubs to give the otherwise bland phrases some sense of importance. I wondered if McDougall was actually dumb enough to take any of the stuff seriously.

I didn't have long to wonder. The door opened and McDougall came in with Mrs. Proctor. He had the sort of vacant smile on his face that gave me an answer — yes, he probably was that dumb. Mrs. Proctor certainly was not. I can't say she was inspired or brilliant or even a very good teacher, but she certainly wasn't stupid. From the glint in her eyes, I had a feeling she was about to use whatever intelligence she had to fix me for good.

"Ian, you're probably wondering why you're here," Mr. McDougall began, still smiling. He managed to slip his considerable bulk behind the small desk.

"Yes."

"Well, it's not as if you're in trouble," he said, laughing, though it didn't seem particularly funny to me. "It's really about a new program that the board is setting up for next year. We think it would be perfect for you."

I looked over at the other part of the "we," Mrs. Proctor.

"You see, Ian," Mrs. Proctor said, "your standardized test scores and the psychological profile that was done in January both indicate that you're quite gifted."

"But I can't hold a pencil straight."

"Well, Ian," McDougall said, "that's the nature of being gifted. You have unusual talents in some areas and perhaps some skill deficits in other areas."

"And there are the socialization problems associated with giftedness," Mrs. Proctor said.

"You mean I don't fit in."

Mrs. Proctor glared at me and I glared back.

"Now, Helen, let me explain," McDougall broke in.

Helen! I thought. This was a face that launched a thousand ships? No wonder she used the initial.

"The gifted program is being designed to give students like you the kind of challenge you're not getting in regular classes. It will give you a chance to work with other gifted youngsters in a small class with teachers who are specially trained to deal with you."

"Sort of like being handicapped?" I asked.

"No, nothing of the sort. The idea is for you to

reach your own maximum potential, Ian." He said this as if he were reading it off one of the posters behind my head. "Someone with your ability — just look at these test scores," he said, pushing forward some graphs. "You shouldn't be studying the traditional ninth-grade novel."

"Maybe the traditional ninth-grade novel shouldn't be *The Outsiders*," I said.

"I agree with you, Ian," Mrs. Proctor broke in. "But that *is* the novel on the course, and though I'd like to assign Camus or Dostoevsky, no one in that class but you and R.T. could read it."

"I guess."

"That's really the whole point, Ian," McDougall said, grinning at me, "working at your proper level."

"I am at my proper level," I told them. "I'm ahead of my proper level, since I skipped fifth grade. My math is terrible — barely passing. I took a shop class once and almost cut off my thumb."

"The gifted class will be able to deal with your exceptionalities better than we can here," McDougall said.

"Suppose I don't want to be gifted."

"Well, I don't know," he said, flustered. This wasn't going as he had planned. "The tests all indicate you have such extraordinary ability . . ."

"But I haven't done much with it, have I?"

"That's right, Ian," Mrs. Proctor said. "We think the gifted class might be a way for you to reach your potential instead of just wasting your talent on personal vendettas."

She looked at me, just to make sure I'd read "Missing Link" in her words.

159

"The vendettas are over," I told her. "You're right about my wasted talent, but that's something I have to fix right here, not in some class where everybody has a label."

McDougall stopped smiling. It was getting serious. "The bottom line, Ian, is that you might fit in there. You don't fit in here."

"Maybe both sides have to change a little, then," I told him. "Maybe I've got to find some way to get along around here." All this time spent waiting for the mother ship, and now the board of education was going to beam me up.

But I didn't want to go.

"You want another year with Donald Fraser?" Mrs. Proctor asked.

"I *need* another year with him," I said. "Maybe I need to tutor some handicapped kids or join a chess club or find some more friends. But I have to do all that right here. I can't just run away from it."

Helen Proctor sighed and looked over to McDougall, who shrugged. There was some more talk about my being able to change my mind, about Rick having to sign some forms, but my mind was made up, and we all knew it. I was staying put.

23
. . . .
Libby

I think we were all nervous waiting for the jury verdict, all of us except Ian, who seemed to be in some kind of continual meditation. The five of us crowded into the courtroom an hour before we had to be there. Rick was in a sport coat and tie specially bought from Goodwill, Vulgaris was wearing a dress I had loaned her and looked fairly sharp, Granny wore her usual suit of silk, and I had my soon-to-be-worn-out MaxMara dress. With the exception of Ian, who refused to put on even corduroys, we looked fairly respectable. I kept praying that the judge would be fooled by the clothing.

But the look on the judge's face when he came in suggested that he probably wasn't fooled by much of anything. My father stood up. The clerk read out the charge. The judge put on some half-glasses to read his decision. Most of the words zipped by without meaning much, but the last phrase made sense: "Hold the defendant not guilty."

And that was it. There was a little grumbling from the half-dozen spectators, a shrug from the prosecutor, and a handshake between my father and the lawyer from the Civil Liberties Union. It was all over, but what did it mean? I had delayed my decision on California for a month waiting for this moment, waiting for things to become clear. But they weren't. Everything was spinning around, messy and confused, like dirty dishwater swirling down the drain.

Nor did Rabbit help much when she called later on.

"Congratulations," she said. The sound was a little mushy because she was probably stuffing her face with some Cheez-Its.

"How'd you hear?"

"Evening news." She chomped. "They had an interview with the prosecutor and some university professors talking about censorship and your dad being some sort of test case."

"Figures."

"Yeah. So I guess you're staying, huh?" Rabbit tried to make this question sound as if it didn't matter to her one way or the other, but I knew it did. Sometimes, when I was really down, I thought Rabbit was the only person who cared about me.

"I don't know."

"Well, you wanted to see how the court case went. And now that your father's innocent, you're not going to cut and run, are you?"

Cut and run; that was Ian's phrase, too. Why did everybody see going to California as running *away* and not running *to* something? Why did it seem so simple to everybody else and so hard for me?

162

"I don't know," I told her. "I've got to think some more."

"You're starting to think too much, Libby. Pretty soon you'll be as bad as your brother."

That was Rabbit. I'd miss her . . . if I left. If . . . That was the decision that was driving me crazy. I tried to sort out reasons and emotions. I made a list. I flipped coins — heads I go, tails I stay. No, two out of three; no, three out of five. Who did I love? Who could I trust? Where was my real life supposed to be? I just couldn't sort it all out.

Somehow I made it through my classes at school the next day, ignoring the whispers and headshaking of the other kids. When it was over, Rabbit met me at my locker, just by the rear gun port. We took a look outside to see if it was still raining, the way it had been dripping all day. I looked at the sky and saw the clouds clearing away. It was Rabbit who looked down.

"There's your brother, in trouble again," she said.

Ian was down in the parking lot with his strange friend R.T. and a small crowd of older kids, mostly seniors. It looked like the crowd was getting ready to stomp the two of them but hadn't quite worked up to it yet.

"That looks like Eddie," Rabbit said, pressing her nose to the glass.

And she was right. At the center of the group facing Ian was Eddie, my former boyfriend. And he was leaning against a car I knew all too well — it was Shelley's.

"Let's go down," I said.

"It could be trouble," Rabbit mumbled.

"Then I'll go myself."

Rabbit followed me as I ran down the four flights of stairs. She was huffing and puffing when we reached the parking lot. I was just angry.

I could feel the tension as we walked over — a fight that wanted to happen, that was building up for the first punch. Eddie was jeering at Ian, egged on by his football buddies. Shelley and Debbie were inside the car, looking bored, as if they were infinitely superior to the little confrontation outside.

"What's going on?" I asked Ian.

"Your friends don't like the court decision," he shot back.

"Libby doesn't have any friends," one of the football players shouted out.

"No human friends," Eddie threw in, "only rabbits."

"And Rabbit's a dog," said another.

I could see Rabbit pull back, ready to run off. These jerks were ripping her up, ripping up anybody who seemed easy to hurt.

"Why don't you rejects go chase a football someplace," I shouted back at them. "That's all you know how to do, anyway."

"You see why I dumped her," Eddie said smugly.

"Why don't you just get out of town," one of the guys yelled at me. "Go off to California where you belong," he said. Then the jeering began.

"Yeah, everybody in California's into porn."

"Maybe Libby can get in the movies."

"Nah, she ain't got the body."

"Her head's too big."

"And nothing else is big enough."

The last line came from Eddie, as if he'd ever got far enough to know.

164

"You jerk," I said, though the words didn't come out very strong.

"And you know what else, guys?" Eddie went on. "If you think Liberty is a funny name, you should hear her middle name!"

I swallowed hard. Why had I ever told him? How could I have been so stupid as to trust someone as phony as that?

"It's Io," he announced. "She's named after a Greek cow!"

"Eee-o, eee-oo," the others began chanting.

I began to feel as Rabbit did. I looked around at their faces, but couldn't find anything to say.

Ian came to my rescue. "Cheap shots," he shouted at them. "That's all you're capable of. Your mouths are like $49.95 Daisy rifles — easy to shoot off but hard to hit anything with. You guys have all the wit and intelligence of a Chef Boyardee meatball."

"Listen to the little freak," Eddie told the others. One of the kids spit on the ground in some kind of gross challenge.

The crowd stared at the three of us — stupidly assured that we didn't belong there, or anywhere decent people lived on Earth. Eddie's jaw was drawn tight, his mouth in a sneer. His friends had folded their arms over their chests, their faces full of righteousness. And Shelley looked out the side window of her car with a little smirk on her face. It was that perfect, bored, self-satisfied expression I had thought so elegant just months before.

But now I saw through it — to the complacency and emptiness and ugliness that was really there. Shelley's smile got me over my embarrassment. It got me angry enough to speak.

"So maybe he is a freak," I told them. "Maybe he doesn't belong with the rest of you. Why would he want to? Why would he want to spend time with a bunch of guys who think the only thing important about a girl is what you can size up with a tape measure?" I was shouting now and looking for new targets. "Why would he want to join a group whose two queens are so bored all they can talk about is themselves and how wonderful they are? You know what's wrong with all of you? You're afraid of anyone who's different. You're afraid of my father and his store. You're afraid of Rabbit and Ian and me, and even little R.T., because we won't buy the lies you all pretend to believe in. And if people like you pass for what's normal around here" — I stopped for breath — "then I'm a freak, too." The words came out without my thinking, and they surprised me, but they were true.

"Me, too," said Rabbit, proudly.

"And me," said R.T.

"And certainly me," Ian agreed.

The four of us were together now, the four of us against all of them. We knew that behind them stood many, many more. A whole school, almost. A whole city beyond that. But I had a feeling that our little group of four was going to grow, that the other side was breaking up even as we stared at them.

Somebody ended the staring contest by pointing at the doorway of the school. The principal, one of the VPs, and Ian's battle-ax English teacher were all walking in our direction. In a second, the crowd of football players began to disappear. Shelley started up the car and roared out of the parking lot, almost knocking Eddie over on the way.

166

"Thanks, Libby," Ian said to me, after the other side had gone. "You were great."

"I just told them the truth," I said.

"That's what made it so good," Rabbit joined in. "I've wanted to say something like that for years."

Little R.T. just stood there smiling, as if I'd saved his life.

"But can you really be happy being a freak here with us?" Ian asked. The question was actually bigger than that, but now the answer was clear.

"You mean, am I going to stay?"

"I guess that's what I really wanted to know," Ian said, looking up at me.

Suddenly the choice was easy — maybe it had been easy all along. "I'm going to stay," I told him. "There's been enough running away in our family. Maybe it's time we stood our ground."

I put my arm around Ian's shoulder as we walked toward home. For the first time in years, he didn't shake it off.